The Abandoned Gold Mine

Rebecca

Babcock

The Abandoned Gold Mine

John C. Souter

Tyndale House Publishers, Inc.
Wheaton, Illinois

Books in the Choice Adventures series

1 *The Mysterious Old Church*

2 *The Smithsonian Connection*

3 *The Underground Railroad*

4 *The Rain Forest Mystery*

5 *The Quarterback Sneak*

6 *The Monumental Discovery*

7 *The Abandoned Gold Mine*

8 *The Hazardous Homestead*

Library of Congress Cataloging-in-Publication Data

Souter, John C.
  The abandoned gold mine / John C. Souter
    p.   cm. — (Choice adventures ; #7)
  Summary: The reader's decisions control the adventures of a group of
children in and around an abandoned gold mine, as they find out more about
themselves and God.
  ISBN 0-8423-5031-4
  1. Plot-your-own stories. [1. Gold mines and mining—Fiction.
2. Adventure and adventurers—Fiction. 3. Christian life—Fiction.
4. Plot-your-own stories.] I. Title. II. Series.
PZ7.S7255Ab   1992
[Fic]—dc20   91-28332

Printed in the United States of America

99 98 97 96 95 94 93 92
 9   8   7   6   5   4   3   2

1

"**L**ook, an old Wells Fargo office. I wonder how much gold went through those doors." Chris made his comment to no one in particular.

The weather-beaten bricks of the assay office had been stuck together in a haphazard pattern with lime instead of mortar. The building dated back to the days of the California forty-niners gold rush.

Todd Winfield just nodded. He'd lived in Nevada City all fifteen years of his life, and talk about gold only bored him. Today he felt like a tour guide. He didn't really know Chris Martin or his younger sister Nancy and their cousin Jill that well. They had flown out to California with Chris's mom to spend a week of vacation with Todd's family. The adults all knew each other "from way back," but this was the first time the kids had ever met.

"Yeah," Todd said, "that's where they weighed the gold brought in from the mines. Then they shipped most of it out to San Francisco—to the mint."

"Hey, look at this!" As everyone turned around, nine-year-old Nancy climbed onto a heavy piece of rusting mining equipment standing next to the road like a sculpture. "What is this thing anyway?" she called down from her perch on top of a weathered beam.

Todd got annoyed. He didn't like "kids," especially the spastic Nancy type. And that went double for kids who

2

climbed on public mining artifacts. "Leave it alone," he told
her. Then he mumbled to himself, "Why did I have to get
assigned to baby-sitting duty?"

Nancy scowled and stayed put.

"Says here it was a stamping machine," Jill said,
reading a sign fastened to the piece of machinery. She
shook her long brown hair back, then glanced at Todd out
of the corner of her eye. Although only thirteen and
younger than the two guys, Jill felt her maturity made up
for her age.

"That's what they used to smash the rock that
contained the gold ore, right?" Chris answered, looking
back to Todd for support. He could just imagine a grizzled
miner leading several burros weighed down with bags of
gold dust coming down the cobblestoned streets.

Todd sighed. "Yeah. Most of the gold had to be
separated from the rock by these stamping machines." He
noticed Jill had stopped reading and was looking over at
him. *Cute,* he thought, *really nice smile.* "This thing used to
be at one of the mines." He feared if he talked too much
about gold, the next thing he knew the Martin kids would
be trying to talk him into going on one of those boring
mine tours.

Nancy suddenly plopped onto the sidewalk in the
middle of their small group. "Hey! I'll bet there must be
some abandoned gold mines we could explore. Maybe we
could even find some ore for ourselves!"

Everyone looked at Todd. Of course, he knew about
the abandoned mines dotting the surrounding hills. He'd
explored his share of them, but he couldn't imagine

leading this gang on such a dangerous expedition. If his parents ever found out he'd taken them into an abandoned mine, it would be "death by methodic removal of all vital organs," as he liked to say.

"Naw. Nothing like that 'round here," he said, doing his best to sound bored.

Jill looked up at Todd, ran her fingers through her long hair, and smiled. "I'll bet you could show us a mine if you wanted to." Dark and dirty tunnels didn't really interest her, but there was one thing she definitely wanted to explore: what made this high school guy tick.

Todd looked at her for a long moment, then at the expectant expressions on the faces of Chris and Nancy. "Well, I do know about one open shaft," he said. "But it doesn't go anywhere, and you'll all be disappointed by it."

"OK, OK, let's go!" Nancy's pigtails flopped against her shoulders as she jumped up and down.

"Sounds good to me, Todd. Where is it?" Chris couldn't feel more ready for a real-life gold mine if he'd thought up the idea himself. He could just picture them discovering some long-lost gold vein that would make them all rich. Besides, he wanted to have a collection of adventures to tell the other Ringers when they all got home.

"Well, it's on the other side of the bridge. But I'm telling you, it's really nothing."

Todd led the group past the old National Hotel, across the bridge over the freeway bisecting town, and back behind the old abandoned brewery. There they discovered a tunnel that was hidden by overgrown weeds and disappeared into the side of the hill.

4

"Pretty neat, Todd. Let's check it out," Chris said as he advanced toward the opening. He didn't need any encouragement to go exploring.

"Uuuuhh, it's not that simple," Todd answered. "You don't have a flashlight. Can't see without a flashlight."

"Yes. Todd's right." Now that they'd seen the mine, Jill didn't really want to go in. After all, who knew what *things* lived in there . . . things that had more than two legs and probably loved long hair. She shivered a little. "It's probably not all that safe, anyway. I think we should go swimming or something instead."

"That's a great idea," Todd replied, a little relieved to hear Jill's change of mind.

"Wait a minute," said Nancy. "We've come all the way across the United States to see this gold mine, and I'm not going home without exploring it—*with or without you!*"

Chris didn't like the idea of agreeing with his bratty sister, but he had to admit that he could hardly wait to go into the open tunnel.

CHOICE ⇒

If the group goes swimming, turn to page 19.

If they go into the mine, turn to page 102.

If Todd talks them into going to Grass Valley, turn to page 51.

"**N**o, wait!" Scotty said, grabbing Todd's arm. "We'd better hide! Quick over here!" The three boys slipped back into the darkness, hiding behind an outcropping of the wall.

"Whatcha gonna do with your share?" one of the men asked.

The other man, the one with the deep voice, laughed. "I'm gonna buy me a whole new life. Nobody in these parts will ever see me again."

The three guys looked at each other. They were afraid to attempt running off—what if the men heard them? As Todd listened to the men talk, he suddenly realized he had heard the deep voice before. But where?

"Man, this stuff is heavy. We'd have been out of here hours ago if this stuff wasn't so heavy."

Chris moved his foot slightly and he knocked over something. It landed in the dark with a thud. The men in the next tunnel suddenly stopped talking.

"You hear something?"

"Naw. Your imagination is working overtime. There's nothing out there."

But one of the men came out with a flashlight in one hand and a gun in the other. He began to check around.

As the light approached their position, Scotty suddenly ran out of the darkness and right past the man,

6

who whirled around and shot into the darkness. Scotty had already disappeared. Todd couldn't believe he had run off like that. Now they would get captured for sure.

"Who's there?" the other man cried, joining the first. Both of them had guns.

"Some punk kid. Let's look and see if there are any more in here."

The light followed the tunnel and came to rest on both Todd and Chris.

"Come out of there, you two!" one of the men snarled.

The two men grabbed Chris and Todd, pushing them into the room where the gold was. When Todd saw the first man, he suddenly recognized him. The guy owned the hamburger stand on East Main Street! As he looked at Todd, he knew they'd met before.

"Now what, boss? They've seen us."

The other man just stared at Todd, who felt like a bug being held by the wings, waiting to be smeared on a microscope slide. He swallowed hard.

"One of them got away."

"But did he see ya?"

"I don't think so."

"Then, we gotta kill these two, boss. They've seen us."

Chris looked up at their gun barrels and closed his eyes. He didn't want to see the bullets before he felt them.

CHOICE

Turn to page 41.

"**Y**ou're not afraid are you?"

"No. But I have no intention of jumping. You want to jump, go ahead. I'll sit here and wait," said Jill.

"OK," he said. And in a minute he leaped out into the pool below. The splash almost reached her up on the hill. It didn't take him more than three minutes to climb back up beside her, his body wet and shivering.

"Felt great."

"I'll bet. That's why you're shivering, huh? You should have brought your towel."

"Yeah." This girl seemed so different from all the other ones he knew. He liked her, but he really didn't know how to act around her. She made him feel funny.

"How come you didn't come out here with your parents?" he said at last.

"I usually spend most of the summer in Millersburg. My parents both work. This year, my dad didn't have any vacation coming, so he figured I might get more out of my summer if I travelled out here with the Martins."

Talking about her parents made her miss them more. She also missed her church. It had been almost two months since she had seen the kids in her youth group, and she realized how much her friends meant to her—especially Betty, her best friend.

"You have any best friends?" she asked.

8

He thought for a moment. "Got a few guys I hang out with—like Frank over in Grass Valley. But I don't really have a best friend."

Too bad, she thought. She and Betty shared everything; nothing could replace a best friend.

"We better get back or the Martins will have a cow."

As it turned out, they weren't having a cow, but Nancy was having a mild allergic reaction to her bee sting. That, plus the fact that they all seemed to be burned to a crisp, made them ready and eager to head home. They figured they could search for gold later, maybe on Saturday.

It had definitely been a fun afternoon.

THE END

Turn to page 143.

Todd looked at Jill. She seemed scared at the strange character they'd come across. Perhaps he could show her how cool he was by showing he wasn't afraid of the guy.

"Nevada, my friends here are from the East Coast. They wanted to meet a real miner."

"Real miner, huh? Well, yer lookin' at one. What ya wanna know?"

Todd could see that this man ate, slept, and drank gold. If anyone had tales to spin, he would.

"What was it like?" Chris said. "Working in the mines, I mean."

The man laughed to himself. "Hard, kid. That's why they call it hard-rocking. Greasy dirt. Bad air. Water drippin' down on you all the time. And cave-ins. Never could be sure when the mountain would dump on ya."

"Why'd you keep working there if the conditions were so bad?" Jill seemed sympathetic.

"Blood. Gets in yer blood. Every man workin' at the bottom of a shaft half believed he'd be rich someday. They made us shower and change clothes after every digging. Didn't want nobody stealing no ore."

"It seems like it would have been such a hard life."

Nevada looked at Jill and gave her a toothless smile. "Maybe we was dummies, but I lived for that hole in the mountain. When they closed the last mine down during

10

the big war, didn't know what to do. Tried hard-rocking in Mexico, but ended up back here. Guess you might say gold's my wife—my partner for life."

Nevada was interesting, but Jill was ready to go. It didn't take much to see that Nevada's life had been consumed by the desire to get rich. She felt pity for him.

Turn to page 49.

"Look, Todd, this is a chance of a lifetime for me," Chris said. "I'll probably never have an opportunity to explore an old gold mine again. If you won't come, I've got to go alone."

"Me, too. I wanna go, too." Nancy didn't want to miss out on anything her brother might do.

Now Todd knew he had really gotten himself into trouble. If he let Chris and Nancy go on by themselves, he'd be forever blamed if they got lost or hurt. He knew his conscience couldn't live with that. He would already be in trouble with his folks if they found out he had taken his visitors this far.

"Look, Todd," Chris began, "let's go back and get some flashlights, jackets, and some food. And maybe even some string so that we can find our way back here. Then it won't be dangerous at all."

"OK, OK, but you have to promise we'll come back," he said. Todd led them back to the mouth of the tunnel and they went back to his house to get flashlights for everybody, jackets, junk food for their pockets, and a ball of string.

But the sun felt so warm, and the sky seemed so blue—Jill could never remember seeing such a blue sky in Washington—she couldn't imagine going back into that cold tunnel.

12

"Todd, why don't we let Chris and Nancy go by themselves. Chris can take care of himself. Besides, I really wanted to go swimming."

Todd hesitated. If he had a choice, he certainly didn't want to spend it in this mine with Chris and Nancy. He would much rather be with Jill anyway. But then, he had to take care of everyone, didn't he?

CHOICE ➤

If they separate, turn to page 78.

If they all go back into the mine together, turn to page 95.

"**J**ill wants to go swimming," Todd said, as he picked up the two-man raft, "so let's all *go swimming!*"

"Wait a minute," Jill said as she lay down on her towel. "When girls say they want to 'go swimming' it isn't because they necessarily want to get into the water. I want to sunbathe, not swim."

Todd looked at Chris. "Did you hear that? She dragged us all down here to *sunbathe?*"

"You mean I skipped exploring a mine so Jill could toast herself?"

Todd dropped the raft, and the two guys began to approach Jill.

"Now, wait a minute, you guys. . . ." She tried to roll away. "You're not going to. . . . No!" They each grabbed an arm and a leg and picked her up, carrying her toward the river. *"Please,* you guys! . . . I can't swim! . . . My hair! You'll mess up my hair! I'm allergic to water! Nooooo!"

Splash!

"Oh, oh! It's *so c-c-cold!"* she said through chattering teeth.

In a moment Nancy came belly flopping in, sending spray over everyone. The two guys jumped back to avoid the water, and then both girls began to splash them mercilessly.

The guys retreated out of the girls' range, then came

charging wildly back and plunging into the shallow water, drenching both girls.

After ten minutes of water fights, Nancy said, "Hey, let's go tubing!"

Nancy got into the inner tube, and the other three grabbed the small raft. After they had launched out into the deep part of the river, Chris and Jill both somehow managed to climb into the small raft; Todd held onto the edge.

They floated down river and through rapids and small riffles. Jill's upper body had dried, and every time they came to another stretch of white water, she would try to stay high in the raft, squealing whenever she got sprayed. She had never done anything like this before.

"This is a blast!" Jill exclaimed.

"You haven't seen anything until you ride on one of the big rivers, like the American over in Placer County. Last summer my family went down the Rogue River up in Oregon. Now *that* was a river!"

Jill thought how much she would love to live in a place like this. It was so fun. Best of all, the heat here was dry, with hardly a hint of the sticky humidity around Washington, D.C.

CHOICE

Turn to page 132.

Chris decided it would be better if he just called his mother. After all, she needed to know what had happened. Because he couldn't remember Mr. Winfield's number, he looked it up in a telephone book in a booth in downtown Nevada City.

Ring! He could hear the telephone ringing, but no one seemed to be home. After several rings, a recorder came on the line.

"This is Brad Winfield. If you would like to leave a message, please wait until after the tone. Thank you."

For a moment Chris didn't know what to do. If he left a message, it would only cause his mother to worry. Maybe it would be better for him to just call 911. He hung up without leaving a message.

CHOICE

Turn to page 122.

16

Finally Mr. Cookson smiled and asked, "From the East Coast? Where 'bouts?"

Todd let out a long breath of relief. Maybe things would work out after all.

"Millersburg, near Washington, D.C., sir," Chris said in answer to Mr. Cookson.

Mr. Cookson smiled. "So you want a look at the vault, eh? Well, why not. Might give you some stories to tell when you go back home."

Mr. Cookson lifted up the countertop so that all four kids could come back into the work area. "Over there you'll notice Sammy working on some jewelry. We do our own gold and silver jewelry here." Sammy looked up and smiled.

Their host pointed to the black barrier at the back left-hand side of the room. "Behind that barrier sits one of my employees. He's got an arsenal of guns just in case anyone tries to come in here and pull off an armed robbery."

He then opened the thick vault door. As they all did their best to cram inside, Nancy's mouth dropped open. "Wowwie. This is *unbelievable!*"

Mr. Cookson smiled at her as he pointed out all of the solid gold bars—gold bullion. He pulled out several drawers full of different denominations of gold coins from many different countries. He also had several bags of gold dust all neatly marked and weighed.

"This must be worth millions!" Chris said in a stunned voice. He had never seen so much gold and silver in all his life. It even rivaled the riches they had seen at the Bureau of Engraving and Printing in D.C. He couldn't wait until he got home to tell the other Ringers that he had been allowed into a gold vault.

Mr. Cookson didn't add to Chris's comment, he just smiled. As they stepped back out of the vault, he pointed out the elaborate alarm system that had been put into the office to keep thieves from breaking into the vault at night. He had all the doors and windows wired and a motion detector rigged to keep anyone from walking through the office to the heavy vault door, which had also been wired.

After their tour, and after expressing their enthusiastic thanks to Mr. Cookson, the gang decided to check out the Holbrooke lobby. The two-story hotel had the same ill-fitting red bricks that marked almost all of the historic buildings in Grass Valley and Nevada City. When they noticed the vending machines in the lobby, everyone got a soda pop, then sat down to decide their next move.

"I just can't imagine having all that gold in that little office," Chris said, shaking his head. "Seems like somebody could just come in there fast, with smoking guns like in the movies, and carry all that gold away."

Jill had to admit the small office did seem to her to be a little more vulnerable than the owner thought. She expected lots of iron bars, armed uniform guards, and a much bigger vault. But right now, her biggest worry was

18

her stomach. "What say we go for hamburgers somewhere?"

They all walked down the street to a fast-food stand, and Todd bought everyone lunch. "Thank my dad," he said when they looked at him surprised.

"That vault was really neat," said Chris. "But I still want to go back and check out that tunnel. Who knows what we might find!"

"Yeah," Nancy added. "I'll bet there has to be some leftover gold in that mine."

Todd could see that they would hound him until he took them into a mine somewhere. Then he remembered Fred. "Hey, I've got an idea. A friend of mine has a real mine shaft all to himself here in Grass Valley. Maybe if he's home we could talk him into showing it to us."

"Yeah, yeah," Nancy jumped at the idea.

"But what about swimming?" Jill asked. She was beginning to wonder if anyone even heard her.

"Jill, we can always do that later—or at home, for that matter. But we can't go into any mines when we get back home. We've just *got* to check out one of those places."

Jill didn't agree with Chris, but she felt outgunned.

"Where does this guy live, Todd?" Chris asked.

Turn to page 71.

"**H**ey, it's so warm outside, it would be a shame not to go swimming." Jill just couldn't wait to get away from the mine.

"We can go swimming anytime back home," Chris complained. "But there aren't any *gold mines* back in Millersburg." He just had to have a good story to lay on the Ringers when they got back home.

"You want gold, huh?" Todd knew he had to make his argument creative. "Let me show ya where most of the gold comes from in this county."

"Where?" Chris sounded skeptical.

"The rivers. More gold is found in the rivers around here than anywhere else. People get lots of real gold out of rivers like the Yuba every day. I'll show you their diggings."

"Let's go, let's go!" Nancy's pigtails flopped again as she jumped.

"But can we swim?" Jill asked. She couldn't care less about looking for gold.

Todd smiled at her. "Sure, let's go back to my place, and we can all get our suits."

The four kids left the mine behind, crossed the bridge, and walked up the curving hill toward the outskirts of Nevada City. The Winfield house sat outside the official city limits, nestled among cedar and pine on half an acre.

After Jill had put on her yellow swimsuit, she stepped

outside to wait for the others. She liked the smell of the forest. Although the Winfields had a lot of property, they didn't have any grass—only dirt covered with wild plants and a layer of brown needles and pinecones.

"Ya like it here?" Todd's words startled her. As she turned, she saw him dressed in cutoffs and pushing a ten-speed bicycle.

"Yes. It's so . . . so *different* from Millersburg."

Todd looked around. The place didn't look that unusual to him. Of course, he had never known anything but the Sierra foothills. "Maybe I could show you my favorite swimming spot."

"I'd like that."

Nancy burst out the front door like a buzz saw, kicking up dust and pine needles as she made her own path underneath the trees. "Let's go, let's go. I'm ready."

When Todd turned to see Chris coming out the front door, he couldn't believe it. Chris had on the gaudiest swim trunks he had ever seen. But even funnier were his white toothpick legs, knobby knees, and feet that looked like they had been in dishwater too long. Had this kid ever seen the sunlight before?

"Man, is that how they dress for swimming where you come from?" Todd couldn't stop laughing.

Chris looked down at himself. "What's wrong?"

Todd just shook his head. "Hey, I'm not sure I want any of my friends to see me with someone who looks like a nerd. You'll need something on your feet. Use a pair of those beach thongs sitting on the porch."

Chris didn't understand the big deal about his

swimsuit. But he figured since Todd was a year older and knew the local customs better, he'd follow his advice. Even so, he sure wished Todd would stop laughing every time he looked in his direction.

"OK, everybody. We're going to the Yuba River, which is a couple of miles, some of it up and down steep hills. So we've got two choices. We can ride bikes if you're up to it, or we can get a ride from my mom."

CHOICE

If the group rides bikes, turn to page 58.

If they go by car, turn to page 135.

22

Chris shrugged, but Nancy whirled around and ran toward the water. So the other three walked uphill toward where the bridge connected with the bank.

"Is this thing safe?" Jill asked. She could see holes in the floor of the bridge.

"Sure. Just be careful where you walk."

Chris liked the feel of the old bridge. The floor creaked, and you could see the boulder-strewn river through the holes. It would be a long fall from here. Several high school kids, already on the bridge, yelled down at friends in the water through a large opening in the bridge's side.

Jill carefully stepped around the small openings; the sight of the rushing river below made her feel queasy.

"I dare you to jump!" said one of the high schoolers to his buddy.

"I'll jump if you do," replied the other guy.

Chris looked down and shook his head. Jump all the way *down there?* You couldn't even tell how deep the water was.

"OK, let's go together," said the first guy. Together both teens stepped into the open space, let go of the bridge sides, and prepared to jump.

Jill didn't want to watch. Why would anyone want to take such risks? It sure didn't make sense to her.

After they jumped, she heard loud horselaughter echo inside the enclosed bridge. She looked up to see that only one of the guys had jumped; the other howled in triumph over his buddy.

"I'm getting hungry," Chris said. "Let's go back."

Nancy shivered as she came up to the blankets. "The water is *cold*. What's to eat?"

Jill opened the picnic basket and passed out sandwiches to everyone. "What do you want to drink, everybody? Got a Coke, a root beer, a Sprite, and a grape soda."

"Oh! Give me the grape," Nancy said quickly.

As they opened their tuna sandwiches, Chris kept swatting at funny-looking bees hovering around them. "What *are* these creatures?"

"Meat bees," Todd said nonchalantly.

"Meat bees? You guys have weird bugs out here in California," said Chris.

"Actually, they're yellow jackets that are attracted to meat, so keep it covered up. They have a mean bite, and they also sting."

Chris kept having to move his sandwich to keep them from landing on it. "These yellow jackets are a *pain*." He finally just stood up and kept moving across the sand to keep them away from his food.

Todd polished off his sandwich, some chips, and a couple of cookies and lay back to soak in the sun. He and the others were just about asleep when—

"Aaahhhhh!!!!" Nancy sprung up from the blanket and began jumping up and down.

"What's wrong?"

She cried and pointed at her upper lip.

"You got stung by a meat bee," Todd announced. Already her lip seemed puffed up. She pointed through her tears to the can and Todd realized what had happened. "It crawled into her can and stung her when she took a drink."

Todd knew how much those stings hurt. "Here," he said. Taking the blue ice pack from their picnic basket, he put it up against her lip. "The pain will die down in a few moments."

CHOICE➤

If they leave because of the bee sting, turn to page 80.

If Nancy gets over it, turn to page 109.

Todd made the decision to try the Snickers tunnel, and all four began to walk that way.

"Why is it I have this scary feeling?" Jill said, as she stayed right at Todd's arm. She had turned off her flashlight to save the batteries, and she now depended completely on his light.

"Come on, there's nothing to be afraid of in here. Especially if we're careful." Why didn't Todd's words encourage her?

"Yeah, there aren't any swamp creatures down here," laughed Nancy.

"Yes, it would be impossible for anything to live in this place." Chris always tried to be logical and reasonable.

Todd stumbled on one of the rail ties and found himself beginning to fall. He stuck his arms out in front of himself to protect himself from the tunnel bottom, but he flew headlong, right past where the floor should have been and continued down, down. As he tumbled in a midair somersault, his brain flashed back to that endless falling sensation he had experienced in many of his nightmares.

"Ecckk!" Todd gasped as he fell into nothingness.

As he disappeared, Jill froze, not knowing what had happened. She could hear his voice growing dimmer as something whisked him away carrying him deep into the bowels of the earth.

26

"Ahhhh!" a scream escaped from her throat.

Splash!

When Todd hit bottom, he landed on his back in cold dark water. Fortunately, instinct had caused him to hold his breath waiting for the impact at the end of his fall, but as he plunged under the water he had to fight his way back to the surface where he gasped in the air.

"What happened?" Nancy cried.

"Todd's fallen. I hear water. Can you see him?" Chris pointed his flashlight beam in Jill's direction. In a moment she had turned on her own as well. As they followed the path of the light they discovered Jill stood right at the lip of a deep pit into which Todd had fallen.

"Todd, you OK?" Chris called down. They could see movement below.

"Yeah. I think so. Just wet and shaking like an earthquake, that's all."

"How are we going to get you out of there?" Jill shivered for Todd, realizing how cold he must be.

Her question resulted only in silence. They had no ropes and he must be at least thirty feet down in that pit.

"Can you climb out?"

"No way, Chris. The sides of this hole are straight up and down. Looks too slippery, anyway."

"What are we gonna do?" Nancy's voice had an edge of panic to it.

"I'll just have to go for help," said Chris. "Can you hold on down there?" Chris feared that Todd might drown while he tried to find a way out. Why had he insisted they come into this tunnel? Fear grabbed at his stomach and began to tie it into a square knot.

"I think so," replied Todd. "Not much to grab hold of. Mostly, I'm treading water. You'll have to try the other two tunnels back at the crossroad. Hurry! I don't think I can last forever."

CHOICE

Turn to page 76.

28

Todd wondered if Chris would ever be cured of his gold fever. "OK, why don't you two pan for gold, and Jill and I will go for a walk."

"OK," Chris said. He picked up the pie tin and walked to a sandy spot on the river.

"Can I help?" Nancy asked, bouncing up behind him. Chris ignored her. Sometimes having a little sister along was a pain.

She just shrugged her shoulders and watched Chris for a minute. He put a handful of gravel in the pan and tried to slosh it back and forth in the water. But either Chris couldn't get rid of the sand, or he lost all of it. He couldn't seem to keep any of the gold dust—if he had any in the first place—in his pan. After about five unsuccessful panfuls, Chris felt frustrated.

"Let me try!" Nancy demanded, and Chris reluctantly handed her the pie tin.

Todd and Jill walked up on the hillside where they could see all the way back up to the bridge.

"This valley sure is beautiful. I don't see very many homes in here."

"Too steep. Plus I think this area is supposed to stay 'wild and scenic.'"

"I think I'd like to live in California someday—when

I'm on my own. I especially like the weather. Does it get humid here?"

"Humid?"

"Yes. You know, muggy? Lots of moisture in the air, like in the bathroom after a hot shower."

Todd shook his head. "No, not really. But I think I know what you're talking about. When I graduated from grade school my family went back to Kansas City—in August. I about died."

Todd noticed Jill scratching her arms. Then he noticed . . .

"Quick, stand up."

"Why?"

"You're sitting in poison oak."

"Eaaak!" Jill cried. "Ohhh, am I going to itch all over?"

"Not if we can get you washed off quick enough. Let's get you back down to the river."

They ran down to the river and washed her off as well as they could.

"What's wrong?" Chris asked.

"Poison oak."

"Uaaah," said Nancy. "How yucky."

Already Jill's arms had little puffy patches on them. It looked as if she would break out in sores in a day or two. Todd would have to get her back to the house.

"We need to get you to the emergency room at the hospital so you can get a quick shot. After that, my mom makes some stuff she calls 'manzanita tea' by boiling manzanita leaves in water. That will help."

They went back up to the bikes and began to walk up to the road. Now the hill stood between them and Nevada

30

City. Fortunately, Todd saw a neighbor come driving along in a pickup and flagged him down.

"Mr. Urke, could you give us a ride back to town? One of my friends just sat in poison oak."

Not only did his neighbor take them back to town, he also dropped them and their bikes at the hospital.

When the kids arrived back at the Winfield house, Todd knew it would be a bad weekend for Jill. If the itching wasn't bad enough, the sores would be. He hoped that she wouldn't be too miserable.

Jill still liked California, even if she wasn't ready for all of it just yet. She had enough memories for at least one week.

THE END

Turn to page 143.

"**O**K, so you wanna go in there. What will you do if that lamp goes out?" Todd didn't like the idea of getting too deep into the shaft without some backup lighting system.

Chris bent and picked up all the matches and the box and put them into his pocket. "I've got all the matches, and look how much kerosene is in this lamp. It's almost full."

"Well, let's just go a little way and see what's there. If we find anything interesting, we can come back with a couple of flashlights."

Jill didn't know if she liked the sound of all this, but she didn't want to be the only one holding back. Even Nancy seemed ready to crawl into that small opening.

Of course, Jill thought, *I could just wait in this chamber . . . by myself . . . without any light. . . .*

"OK, let's go," she said.

"Let me lead," Todd said, taking the lantern. "We'll just go a little way into this shaft to see where it goes."

Todd crawled for about ten feet before the narrow space opened into something larger. He held out the lamp in front of him and could see it opened into a regular mine tunnel. Tracks meant for the old mine cars ran along the tunnel floor. He stepped into the bigger opening and held up the lantern while waiting for everyone else to climb out.

"Where are we?" Nancy asked.

"We're in one of the old mines."

32

"Look at these tracks. Where do you suppose they lead?"

"Probably nowhere. All of the old mines have been closed down except for the ones that are part of the two mine museums. There's probably no way out regardless of which way you go."

"It has to lead somewhere." Chris seemed determined to go on.

"Yeah, we might find some leftover gold," said Nancy.

Jill couldn't believe Nancy's immaturity.

"To continue on would be very dangerous," said Todd. "We've got to go back. If we go on we have a good chance of getting lost, and no one would ever know where we were."

"These tracks have to lead somewhere."

"Chris, there are *hundreds* of miles of these underground tunnels running under the towns of Nevada City and Grass Valley and the surrounding hills. We could walk for miles and not come to the opening on the surface, and if we did, there's no guarantee that it would still be open. We could easily die down here."

CHOICE

Turn to page 11.

They finally agreed it might be fun to go down under Main Street. So they turned left and started walking into the tunnels.

Scotty explained where air shafts came out and how he and his brother had figured out pretty much where they were. But he hadn't been down in the tunnels for months.

"This is neat, Scotty. You learned about this place all by yourself?" asked Nancy.

"Well, just me and Frank."

Nancy and Scotty seemed to be getting along pretty well. Todd thought to himself, *Birds of a feather flock together.*

"This is underneath the liquor store," said Scotty. "That tunnel there runs up East Main under the Holbrooke."

"Let's go that way," Chris suggested. "We've all been in the Holbrooke."

As they started in that direction, Todd suddenly stopped everyone. "Did you hear something?"

"Hear what?"

"I thought I heard some noises." Todd was sure he had heard something.

"Maybe you're hearing something from the street above," Jill suggested.

"Can't be," said Scotty. "We're too far down in the ground to hear anything from up there."

34

They continued walking, but Todd stopped everyone again.

"Listen," he said, "don't you hear it?"

Now everyone could hear the noises. Talking. Picks against rock. Then talking again.

"Someone's in the mine," Scotty whispered.

Turn to page 106.

Jill heard Todd gasp for air again. She felt so helpless; if it wouldn't have hurt him, she probably would have burst into tears long ago.

"Hold on, you're gonna make it," she said, trying to sound as reassuring as she could.

"Can't . . . so tired. . . ." She could hear his voice quiver. He had taken off his jacket; it only weighed him down in the water. She knew he must be frozen down there.

"Todd, you've *got to* hold on!"

She saw him go under.

"TODD!"

He came up again, gasping for air.

Just then, Jill thought she heard something from the tunnel behind her.

"Todd! Help's coming. Hold on!"

He didn't say anything. But she knew he wouldn't last long.

Jill listened again—there were voices! Strange but beautiful voices echoed down the tunnel.

"Down here! We're down here!"

In a moment she could see light coming her way. For the first time all day she felt a warm sensation around her body.

"Here, we're here!" she said as a man walked up to

her with a light on his head. Behind him came three more rescuers. "Todd's down there, in that hole." She pointed down.

The first man looked over into the pit. "Quick, the rope." In a moment they had secured the rope and had thrown it down to Todd.

"Can you grab it, son?"

Todd made a feeble attempt to hold on to the rope, but he didn't have much energy left.

"Hold on, son. We're coming down for you."

They rigged up one of the men and lowered him down into the pit. When he reached Todd, he hooked another harness around him, and the men at the top slowly pulled him up.

Todd was shivering uncontrollably. They immediately wrapped him in dry blankets and put him on the stretcher. Now they had to work on controlling his hypothermia.

When Chris and Nancy saw the rescuers bring Todd out of the tunnel, followed by Jill, they both jumped for joy. It looked like everything would be all right after all. The Ringers and Nancy watched as the ambulance took Todd to the hospital. Then they all climbed into the car of one of the rescuers, who drove them home. Chris was never happier to be home, but he wasn't looking forward to what his parents would have to say.

THE END
Turn to page 143.

"**W**ell, we're here!" Todd said with a grin, getting off his bike.

Jill took one look at the water and the rocks below the high concrete bridge and shook her head. "How are we going to swim here? There's no beach."

"This way." Todd led them all down the path that went down to the river. "There's a small sandy beach not far from here."

Each of the four walked with their bicycles until they reached an area of white sand surrounded by rocks and granite cliffs. The white water pushing through the small canyon seemed to be moving even faster as they got closer.

As Jill laid her towel down, she looked at the raging water. The river looked pretty fast to her. "You sure you can swim in that?"

"You think this is bad, ya ought to see the Yuba in June when the snow runoff is really rushing through. Kinda calm now." He pointed up river. "There's a couple of pools up there if ya want."

Jill lay down on her blanket. The sun felt good. She gazed up into a dark blue sky like none she'd ever seen before back East and looked at the impressive valley scenery.

"Hey, where's all this gold you told us about?" Chris said, as if he hadn't had enough adventure for one day.

38

"Let's go swimming!" Nancy ran to the water and attacked it with her entire body. In a millisecond she stood right back up. "Ahhh! This is *COLD!*"

Todd enjoyed hearing the brat's squeals when she felt the melted snow water. "Why don't we lie down in the sun for a while, or maybe you could even go swimming," he said, spreading his towel next to Jill's. "Then I'll tell you all about the gold."

"Just point me to where the gold is," said Chris.

CHOICE ⇛

If Chris sits down on the sand, turn to page 126.

If Chris insists on looking for gold, turn to page 63.

"Let's get out of here," Todd repeated in a tense whisper to Scotty.

The younger kid knew just what to do. He immediately went off into the maze of tunnels, which he knew like the back of his hand. Todd and Chris followed him. Unfortunately, the men had heard them, and they were following, too.

"I can hear them behind us," Chris said, out of breath.

The boys came to a fork in the tunnel. "Which way?"

Scotty stood for a moment, trying to decide. "That's a dead end," he said pointing to the right. "That way," he pointed to the left, "leads back to the East Main Street area. We missed the tunnel I wanted."

They could hear the men coming after them.

"Let's try the left," Todd whispered. "At least it's not a dead end."

They turned down the tunnel, and Todd sensed that it must be curving back in the direction from which they had just come. But at least he didn't hear the thieves behind them anymore.

"Wait. We're getting close to where we started."

"I don't hear anyone," said Chris. "They're probably out chasing us."

Scotty led them right past the opening into the Holbrooke and out toward the surface. He had guessed the location where the men entered the mine. They came to a trapdoor that he knew opened out into the alley behind Josie's Cafe.

"Look," Chris said, picking up a gold Krugerrand next to the wooden door. He recognized the South African coin—it was like the ones they saw in the Gold Exchange. The thieves must have dropped it here.

Scotty opened the trapdoor, and the three kids pushed out into the night air.

"Andy?" said a man's voice from the darkness.

In a moment a flashlight beam came on and shone on the boys.

"Stop, you kids, or I'll shoot!"

CHOICE

If they stop, turn to page 141.

If they run, turn to page 124.

"**N**o. Let's just tie 'em up. Use the rope."

Chris opened his eye just enough to peek out.

"You sure?" the second man was saying with a frown. "What if they identify us?"

"We'll just put them someplace where *no one will ever find them.*"

Chris shivered. He wished he'd never even heard about gold mines. If only they had all just gone swimming. How would his parents and his sister feel when they never heard from him again? Would anyone ever know the truth?

Scotty finally reached the rope leading up to his backyard. He all but flew up it. When he reached the surface, he stopped and caught his breath.

Now that he had escaped, he wondered what he should do. If he woke up his mother, she would probably be very upset. And she might not even believe him. But if he didn't get her help, what would happen to Todd and Chris? He finally decided that he had no choice but to wake her.

The two men tied Chris and Todd up, then blindfolded them and led them somewhere deeper into the mine. Todd feared this might be the end for them. Why had he come back into the mine without telling anyone where they were going? In the back of his brain, he hoped Scotty might get help. But by the time help arrived, the

men and their gold would be gone—and no one would
know where to find him and Chris.

Before long, the men took off Chris's and Todd's
blindfolds, but it really didn't matter. The men had turned
off the lights on the boys' helmets, and it was pitch black
except for the flashlight one of the men held. If only they
could get one of their helmet lights turned on after the men
left.

The men gave the boys a hard shove forward, and
they both stumbled then fell onto the hard ground. They
heard the men laughing as they walked away, taking the
only bit of light with them as they left. Soon the boys were
in total darkness.

"Chris, are you OK?" Todd spoke quietly.

"Are we going to die in here?" he asked with a
shaking voice.

"No. We'll get out, somehow. Can you move your
fingers?"

"A little."

Todd bent over and tried to move his head toward the
sound of Chris's voice. "See if you can use your fingers to
turn on my helmet light. Can you feel it?"

Todd's helmet fell off his head and hit the ground.
Chris hadn't been able to grab the light with his fingers. But
Todd could feel the helmet with his knee. He twisted
around, positioning his body so that his free fingers could
feel for the lamp.

"There!" The light came on, and the two boys looked
at each other with relief.

"Hey, Todd, I've got a pocketknife in my pocket. Maybe you could reach in my pocket and get it."

It took Todd quite some time to position himself so that his free hand would be opposite the pocket in which Chris had the knife. As he tried to slip his fingers in the tight jeans pocket, he realized his fingers just didn't have enough freedom of movement to grab it. He felt so frustrated—he could touch the knife, but he couldn't get it out!

"Why don't you try to move it up to the top of my pocket from the outside?" suggested Chris.

CHOICE

If Todd takes Chris's suggestion, turn to page 82.

If Todd thinks it won't work, turn to page 98.

44

"**L**et's go toward the exit first," said Chris. "Then we'll know about two ways out—just in case."

They walked in the direction of the opening to Alta Street. After they had traveled for some time through a maze of tunnels, they finally reached the opening that came up in a vacant field. But a metal grate had been locked over the hole.

"You mean we can't get out here?" Jill asked.

"Doesn't look like it," Todd replied.

"This wasn't here the last time I came this way," said Scotty. "But that was a while ago."

They retraced their steps and walked back toward Scotty's place. When they arrived at the foot of the rope ladder, everyone had a different opinion about what to do next.

"Let's go the other way, underneath the downtown buildings. OK?" Chris said. "Scotty said this way isn't that far."

"But my feet hurt," Nancy complained.

"I'd still just rather go swimming," said Jill.

CHOICE ➡

If they go downtown, turn to page 33.

If they go swimming, turn to page 116.

"Let's try the Snickers tunnel. I'm sure this is the way we came."

Chris and Nancy walked up the tunnel following the tracks for quite some distance when Chris lost sight of the two shiny metal strips.

"What wrong?" Nancy asked.

"I don't see the tracks anymore."

Nancy didn't understand the problem. The tracks had to be there. She stepped around Chris and followed the beam of her own flashlight for a few steps before she lost her footing.

"Nancy!"

At the moment she fell, Chris suddenly realized why they couldn't see any tracks up ahead. They had come to the edge of a drop-off!

Frantically he grabbed at Nancy as her flashlight went flying out into the black hole. He just managed to grab one of her arms as her body fell into the empty place and then against the side of the hole.

"Chris! Help!"

"I've got you!" He had dropped his own flashlight when lunging for her arm. The flashlight fell beside him, then went out. In another second, Nancy's light splashed into some black water far below.

Chris and Nancy were in almost pitch darkness.

Nancy dangled over the deep shaft, and Chris held her skinny arm with all his strength.

His face peered down into the hole as he hung over the side using both hands to keep her from disappearing into the abyss. He could see just a weak spot of light somewhere below from her flashlight and knew the hole had to be about thirty or forty feet deep. Other than that, he couldn't see anything.

"Chris! Save me!"

He pulled with all his might, but he couldn't seem to get any traction with his feet. Finally he managed to get her back up over the edge by bracing his feet against the iron rails. When she came up, she sprawled over on top of his lap, and they both cried thanksgiving prayers to God for saving her.

They sat panting for a few minutes trying to catch their breath. "What do you think, Nance—did we come this way?" Chris was trying to comfort Nancy with a joke, but she just clung to her brother and sobbed uncontrollably. He held her tightly. He too cried as he thought about almost losing her down that hole. He drew her close, feeling protective of his precious little sister. *Oh Lord, please protect her,* he prayed, rocking her.

It dawned on Chris at this moment that he was like a father to Nancy, since their real father was dead. He had never thought of that before. He felt scared and thankful at the same time. *Thank you, Lord Jesus,* he prayed. Nancy slowly calmed down.

Chris felt around and found his flashlight. He turned it off, then on.

Nothing.

He shook it, and fortunately the light once again came back on.

"Come on, Nance. Let's get out of here. This definitely isn't the way we came in."

Turn to page 100.

48

Chris had definitely been wrong before, so he decided to go with Nancy's choice. They started down the Hershey's tunnel.

The tunnel started going downhill, and Chris stopped dead in his tracks.

"I know this is wrong. We never came up a grade this steep. Let's turn around."

Nancy didn't complain, so they retraced their steps and came back to the intersection once again.

"This time let's go into the tunnel with the Nestlé Crunch wrapper. That's got to be the right one."

CHOICE

Turn to page 93.

All the way back up the trail, Chris couldn't stop talking about how much fun it must have been to dig in one of those mines. "I only wish we had gone in that tunnel you told us about. Maybe we could still go back there and explore a little."

Todd wondered if Chris would ever be able to see what gold fever did to people. He had seen the same kind of crazy attitudes in people who drove up Highway 80 almost every weekend to the state of Nevada where gambling was legal. Almost always they came back broke, but they knew someday they'd hit a jackpot. Gambling fever, gold fever . . . didn't seem to be much difference between the two.

Finally they reached their bikes, unchained them, and started back up to Nevada City. Todd knew they would have to walk up a good percentage of the hill ahead of them. Chris seemed deep in thought.

"When we get back, I'm gonna see if Mom will let me call back to Millersburg. I just can't wait to tell Willy and Sam and the others all about what I've seen here."

"Gonna tell 'em how you missed the turn and made a three-point landing?" Todd cracked.

"I don't know. I may skip that part."

Everyone laughed, and Chris knew he'd remember these bruises for a long time.

50

THE END

Turn to page 143.

"Look," Todd said impatiently, "if we go in here, I'm sure we'll be violating some law. I mean, after all, all these mine shafts belong to somebody. 'Sides, my parents will kill me if they find out we went into a place like this."

"I think he's just afraid," Nancy said matter-of-factly.

Todd shot her a look designed to freeze a polar bear. Then he went on, "Listen, I've got a compromise. Let's go over to Grass Valley, and I'll see if my friend at the Gold Exchange will let you see all the gold in his vault."

Chris perked up. "Really? You think we could get into the vault?"

"Why not? He's shown it to me before."

"Awesome!" said Chris.

"How boring," said Jill. She had hoped that they would go swimming. But Chris and Nancy seemed eager to go with Todd to Grass Valley instead of going into the mine. At least Jill didn't have to worry about running into some weird creepy-crawly thing in that dark and dirty place.

The kids located a shuttle bus that was heading in the direction they wanted and got on. When they arrived, Todd immediately took them into the Gold Exchange, which was located in the historic Holbrooke Hotel. Everyone was wowed by all the gold in the glass display cases facing the door. Gold nuggets, gold and silver coins, and all sorts of jewelry sat right there on display.

When Mr. Cookson, the owner, looked up, Todd held his breath. Would he be willing to let them see the vault? Todd would look stupid if he didn't like the idea of letting all these visitors see his hidden wealth.

"Hi, Todd," Mr. Cookson said. "How's your dad?"

"Fine, Mr. Cookson. He's fine. . . . Ah . . . I was wondering . . . I've got these friends with me from the East Coast . . . and I was wondering if they . . . could . . . sort of, like . . . see your vault—like you showed me."

Mr. Cookson stood there expressionless.

CHOICE ➔

If the group sees the gold, turn to page 16.

If they can't see the gold, turn to page 87.

But if Todd yelled at the others to run, and they didn't do it, he'd likely get the man shooting. He might be responsible for getting his friends killed. Maybe it would be better to see what this guy would do.

They reached the trees, and the guy raised his gun. "I ain't killing no kids. When I shoot I want you to fall down," the man said in a low voice.

"What?" Chris said.

"You heard me. When I shoot, fall to the ground and *don't move!*" Immediately the gun went off.

Bang! Bang! Bang!

Instantly, the three kids fell down. Todd hadn't been hit, but he dared not move. He stayed on the ground motionless, heart racing, until the man ran back to the waiting plane, and it took off into the early morning sky.

"You guys OK?" Chris asked at last.

"Yeah," said Todd and Scotty together, finally getting the courage to move.

"Were we lucky, or were we lucky?" said Scotty.

"Luck had nothing to do with it, dudes!" Chris replied, beaming and jumping up. "I prayed that God would protect us, and *yowza*, did he do it or what!" Chris was so overcome with glee that he started hopping around. "I feel like Shadrach, Meshach, and Abednego!"

They went back to the airpark tower and used the

54

pay telephone to call the police and their parents. Though
they hadn't been able to stop the burglary, they were
simply glad to be alive and able to tell of their incredible
experience. Todd figured he'd be a hero at school when
they heard what happened; he wondered if Jill would be
impressed that he almost got killed. Chris couldn't stop
talking about how neat it was that God protected them.
And Scotty—well, for once Scotty didn't know what to say.
He was still trying to figure out what "shed-racks,"
"me-shacks," and "bend-egos" were.

THE END

Quite a bit of excitement for a mere vacation! If you still
haven't seen the mine, turn to page 1 and make different
choices along the way.

Or, turn to page 143.

"**L**ook," Todd said, "why don't you all sit here for a second, and I'll go up the left shaft and check it out. You should still be able to hear me. Either way, I'll come back, and we'll find the way back to the candy bar wrappers."

Jill wanted to go with him, so they turned off her flashlight to save the batteries and started up the left-hand tunnel. They walked for quite some time before they came to another four-way intersection.

"I don't see any candy bar wrappers. Do you think we've made a mistake?" Jill shivered uncontrollably again.

"Yeah. This must be the wrong shaft. We've got to go back to where we left Chris and Nancy and go up the right-hand tunnel."

They walked back down the tunnel for quite some time, calling out as they went. They couldn't hear anything but the echo of their own voices. After they went downhill for a while, they discovered that their current tunnel disappeared once again under water.

"We're lost! Now we can't even find the others. We're going to die down here for sure!"

"Jill, you've got to keep your head. We'll make it. I'm telling you we'll all make it."

They turned around and walked back the way they came.

Everything looked exactly the same. Todd had never

been in such a situation before. He realized how deadly these mine shafts could be. He knew now that the chances that they could find their way back to the others and the original entrance grew smaller with every passing moment. He only hoped they could get to the surface somehow and send a rescue team back for Chris and Nancy.

They walked on and on. With each new turn they seemed to get more confused and mixed up. Todd felt their only hope remained in somehow finding a way out. But he knew that they could easily wander like this forever.

Meanwhile, Chris and Nancy sat at the intersection, listening and waiting.

"They must have gotten lost." Chris knew now that they wouldn't be coming back.

"You think they could have fallen into a hole or something and need us?" Nancy had an active imagination.

"There's nothing we can do for them now. We've got to take care of ourselves. If that had been the correct way, they would have found it pretty quick and come back for us. So the only thing we can do is go to the right because they went to the left."

Nancy complained, but her brother insisted on getting started back. They went up the right-hand tunnel, and soon they came to the candy bar intersection. At least they knew that the Hershey's tunnel didn't lead them back.

"It was either the Snickers tunnel or the Nestlé Crunch tunnel that we came in."

CHOICE

If they follow the Nestlé Crunch tunnel, turn to page 100.

If they follow the Snickers tunnel, turn to page 45.

"**B**icycles. That's the way we should go." Chris didn't like the idea of having to depend on Todd's mother. With bicycles they could come and go as they pleased.

"Yeah, yeah! Let's get going." Nancy didn't seem to have any speed but overdrive.

"How steep did you say those hills are?" Jill hadn't been on a bike in a long time and didn't like the idea of pushing herself too hard.

"Well, it won't be so bad *going,* it's almost all downhill. But you'll definitely feel it when we come back."

"Where's your spirit of adventure, Jill?" Chris asked. He knew any of the Ringers would make the most out of this California adventure.

"Come on, let's do it!" Nancy cried.

Todd let Nancy use his old bike (which had a lot of miles on it). He loaned Chris his older brother's ten-speed, and he gave Jill a new girl's bike that he borrowed from next door. But he kept his own bike for himself.

Todd led the group out onto the highway, and soon they came to the valley through which the Yuba River flowed. He pulled to a stop and steadied himself by putting his left foot on a large rock beside the road.

"Gets pretty steep here, so make sure you all gear down. I don't want to see anyone going off the edge of the road. Pretty steep drop-offs in some places."

"You sure this is safe?" Jill asked, concerned.

"Come on!" said Nancy, impatient as usual. She started off on her own.

"Just shift like me and stay right behind me. OK?"

"Well, if you say so."

Todd smiled back at Jill and then started off. He hoped Nancy wouldn't get herself going so fast that she'd panic on some sharp curve. He could still see the little brat down below.

They hadn't gone far before Chris zipped past them yelling about how slow they were going. Todd sure hoped that city kid knew how to control his brother's bike.

Chris hadn't gone this fast on a bicycle in years. But no matter how fast he went, he couldn't seem to catch Nancy. The road kept getting steeper, and the green trees whizzed past him in a blur. He wobbled a bit coming around a sharp curve, and his confidence suddenly disappeared. He could see up ahead that the road cut back again, and he knew instantly that his current speed would make him lose control.

Frantic to stop, he tried to brake by backpedalling, but his feet only spun around. He didn't have any brakes! He could hear Todd yelling something from behind him. "Hand bra—!"

The corner came upon Chris too quickly. He only tried to turn at the last moment, which snagged his front wheel against the edge of the blacktop lip, causing his bike to stop dead and sending him soaring over the handlebars straight out into dead air.

From behind, Todd watched it happen as Chris flew

off the bike and must have sailed a hundred feet down the hill. He watched what seemed like a slow-motion video as the airborne kid with the bright shorts hit several pine branches before glancing off the side of the slope and disappearing out of his view, continuing down into a maze of tangled manzanita bushes.

"Chris!" Jill couldn't believe it. "Chris! Are you all right?" She and Todd rolled to a stop and peered down the steep bank toward the bushes. Chris lay sprawled, face down. He wasn't moving. Todd stood frozen, not knowing what to do. He looked down the steep gravel-filled slope knowing it would be just about impossible for him to climb down it without falling.

"Do something! Todd, we have to do something!" Jill said, her voice shaking.

CHOICE ➡️

If Todd climbs down to Chris, turn to page 90.

If they get help for him, turn to page 113.

"That sounds neat!" Nancy bounced up. "I want to do that. Let's go."

Todd looked at Jill. She shrugged her shoulders as if to say, "Whatever they want to do is OK with me."

"Let's do it."

They left the radio station, and Todd led the group to the shuttle bus that would take them out to the Empire Mine. There they toured the house the foreman used to live in that had been turned into a museum. They also waited around for the three o'clock tour down into some of the underground tunnels.

"That was neat!" said Nancy as they exited the mine. "I sure wish we'd been alive during the days of the forty-niner gold rush. We could have struck it rich, too!"

"You know who really made the most money?" Jill said. "It was the guys who sold supplies to the miners. That's when Levi's were invented. This guy decided the miners needed clothes that would last, so he made pants out of tent canvas."

Nancy looked skeptical. "How do you know that?"

"Jill's a history freak, remember?" Chris said.

"Let's go home and get lunch," said Todd. "You've seen your mines, and I'm hungry." With that, the Millersburg natives began to forget their gold fever and to

62

yearn for dinner. The group made their way back to Todd's house.

THE END

Have you been to the mine yet? If not, turn back to the beginning and make other choices along the way.

Or, turn to page 143.

"**A**ll right, all right. But let me warn you that if we come on someone's claim, they might be toasting us with bullets."

"Why?" Jill asked, surprised.

"Miners are like pit bulls. Think everybody is gonna rip 'em off. Paranoid, ya know. Anyway, we have to walk softly around any claims we come upon. OK?"

Everyone agreed, so Todd led them over to chain their bikes to a couple of large trees. Then they started down river. When Nancy saw the others were leaving, she grabbed her towel and followed them.

Todd led the group down the path for several hundred yards. As they walked, they could barely hear the sound of a motor running above the roar of the river. Todd pointed ahead. They could see a man in a wet suit in the cold river with a long hose running from what looked like a small boat.

"What's he doing?" Jill asked.

"Dredging the bottom. That hose he's got is like a vacuum cleaner; he sucks up all the sand and small rocks on the bottom and in the cracks. Then they run it through a sluice box."

Another man was working up on the bank. When he saw the four kids he looked up for a long moment before returning to his work. Jill could see a rifle propped against a large rock. She shivered.

"What's a *sluice box?*" Chris asked.

"It's a box that has water running through it," Todd explained. "The water separates the light sand from the heavier gold. It has riffles in it to catch the gold and acts like a gold pan—only it's much bigger and faster."

"Haven't they gotten all the gold out by now?" asked Nancy.

Todd looked at her for a moment. "You'd think so, but there always seems to be more of it washed down the river. The pickings get leaner, but there always seems to be some pickings."

Once, at a county fair, Chris had learned how to use a gold pan. When he realized that gold still sat at the bottom of the rivers here, it made him want to do a little panning himself.

They continued down the trail next to the river. After a while, they stepped on some trash, including a disposable aluminum pie tin. That gave Chris an idea.

"Hey, why don't we try to pan some of that river sand ourselves? Who knows what we could find?" Chris could see visions of gold in his head.

CHOICE ➡

If they pan, turn to page 28.

If they go down the river, turn to page 119.

As they approached the end of the runway, Todd couldn't control himself any more. He suddenly yelled, *"RUN!"* and took off into the bushes.

Bang! Bang! Bang!

The gunman stopped firing after three shots and ran back to the airplane, which had taxied to the end of the airpark's runway. In just a few moments, the Cessna went down the runway and took off into the dawn.

Chris looked around. He didn't seem to have been hit, but when he fell into the bushes, he had wondered for a while. "Todd, Scotty? You guys OK?"

"I'm all right," said Todd.

"Me, too," Scotty answered. "That was *close.*"

They walked back to the airpark tower building and used the telephone to call the police. It didn't take the police long to confirm that the burglary had actually taken place.

Chris had memorized the number printed on the wing of the airplane, and he gave that to the police. They said they'd send out a bulletin to all the airports within the Cessna's range.

With the descriptions the boys were able to provide, the police identified who the thieves were and sent the information to the FBI. They said it would just be a matter of time before the men were captured.

66

Chris couldn't wait to get back to Millersburg and the other Ringers. Would he have a story to tell them!

THE END

Turn to page 143.

They decided to go to the Gold Exchange to check out Nancy's rock.

When they all made it back to the surface, Nancy hummed with admiration for her big rock. "Look how this thing sparkles. I'll bet it's worth millions of dollars!"

Todd just shook his head. He knew that gold prices were based on weight, and even if that entire rock was solid gold, he knew it couldn't be worth millions.

The four caught the shuttle bus to take them over to Grass Valley. Only three miles separated the two towns, but the shuttle wound around among the pine trees and the newer mountain-style homes in between until it finally came to a stop in front of the Holbrooke Hotel.

When they got off, Jill looked up at the two-story building. It looked just like the buildings she had seen in so many movies.

Instead of going into the hotel lobby, Todd led the group into a business off the street in the lower part of the hotel. The small lobby area of the Gold Exchange was encircled with glass display cases filled with various types of gold.

"Wow. Gold coins. I didn't know they made gold coins anymore." Chris dropped open his mouth as he saw all the shiny gold coins from places like South Africa, Canada, and China.

"Look at all these nuggets!" Nancy squealed. "They are in such funny shapes." She couldn't wait to see how much money her rock would be worth.

Jill's attention went to all the gold jewelry. An artisan worked carefully behind the counter putting together a fancy necklace.

While they looked at the gold, the bell on the door behind them sounded, and in walked a stringy-haired man with a gray beard. He plopped a small white bag on the glass counter. Chris noticed a pistol handle poking out of the waist of his dirty jeans. When the man glanced at him Chris felt a chill go up his back from the guy's icy glare.

"Hey, Nevada. Haven't seen you for five weeks." The shop owner stood and came to the counter. "How's your luck been running?"

Nevada poured out the contents of his small bag onto one of the trays of a scale. The man behind the counter began to put different sized weights on the other tray.

"Price of gold is up since you brought in your last poke. Looks like you've got . . . $1,525."

The backwoods man smiled, looking toward Chris with a grin that revealed two missing front teeth. He licked his lips while the owner counted out his money, then he crammed the bills inside his shirt. His hand felt for the handle of his pistol before he approached the outside door and his eyes shifted back and forth as he stepped back into the street.

Watching this transaction had Nancy squirming. She produced her rock and placed it on the glass counter.

"Hi, Jack. My friend here from the East Coast wants to see if there is any gold in this rock she found."

Jack looked at Todd, then at the rock. He held it up for a moment. "Where'd you get this?"

Before Nancy could open her mouth, Todd spoke quickly. "Ah, she just found it lying around somewhere." Todd felt too guilty to admit that they had been down in one of the abandoned mine shafts.

"Looks like it might be from one of the mines," Jack commented as he turned it over in his hand. "Don't get much hard rock anymore.

Mostly we just see nuggets and dust from the rivers."

"Isn't that gold?" Nancy said, pointing to the shiny spot that had first attracted her.

"That's iron pyrite, miss."

"Iron . . . what?"

"Fool's gold."

Nancy's face fell. "I don't get it."

"Fool's gold looks like gold, but isn't. Of course, it often tells you there's gold somewhere near. But can't really say you've got much here. It would probably have to be crushed before you could tell anything for sure." He handed the rock back to her. "At least you've got a nice souvenir for yourself to take back east."

"Well, so much for our great gold strike," Chris said as they stepped back out onto the sidewalk. "I'm hungry."

Although she knew it must be close to five o'clock, Jill wondered if there would ever be enough time for them to go swimming.

THE END

Fool's gold isn't the only thing Jill and Nancy could have found below the surface of this old mining town. If you haven't been under Main Street with the Ringers, turn to page 1 and make different choices along the way.

Or, turn to page 143.

Todd led the group over to Richardson street and up the block to an old Victorian home. "This is my friend's place. Let's see if he's home." Todd lifted the door knocker.

"Where's the mine? It can't be here," Nancy said, looking around.

Before Todd could answer, the door opened, and a little blond kid looked out at them.

"Hi, Scotty," said Todd. "Is Frank home?"

"Nope. He went on a waterskiing trip for the weekend. They won't be home till tomorrow. Who are these guys, Todd?"

"Friends from the East Coast. Chris, Nancy, Jill, this is Frank's brother, Scotty. Hey, we were just wondering about your tunnel; think we could take a look inside?"

Scotty lit up. *"Sure!* I know where everything is."

When Todd saw Scotty's reaction, he wondered if he'd made another mistake. All he needed was another kid acting just like Nancy.

Scotty took them into the backyard and lifted the wooden door covering the hole. They could see a rope ladder going down into it. Scotty told how they had discovered a small hole one summer in the grass. When they dropped rocks into it, they guessed it must lead into one of the mines. So he and his brother had dug down into it and had found a mine tunnel.

"Your father let you do that?" Jill asked. She knew her parents would never have let her open up a hole like this.

"My parents are divorced. Mom doesn't care what we do."

"This tunnel's halfway safe 'cause Frank and Scotty know where most of the shafts go."

"Well, what are we waiting for?" Nancy said gleefully.

"Let me get our spelunker equipment," Scotty said, running to the shed.

"Spelunker? What's he talking about?" Jill arched her brows.

"That's what they call cave exploring stuff."

"Oh."

Scotty came back with three hard hats with lamps on them. He and Todd and Chris all put them on. One by one they all climbed down the rope ladder. The guys held it tight at the bottom so the girls could come down more easily.

"Cold in here."

"Which way you wanna go? We can go back to an exit up on Alta Street, or we can go down under all the buildings on Main Street."

CHOICE ⇒

If they go to Alta Street, turn to page 44.

If they go downtown, turn to page 33.

"**H**ey look," Jill said, crossing her arms and facing the others. "We've spent a lot of time in this stupid mine and almost got lost. Let's do something I want for a change."

Chris had to admit that he hadn't been thinking about Jill, or anyone else for that matter. "OK. But where should we go?"

"It's kind of late to go all the way out to the river," said Todd. "After we change into our swimsuits, we can go over to Pioneer Park where they have a big public pool."

So all four went back up to Todd's house. Nancy kept looking at her rock and wishing it to be worth millions. It didn't take long before everyone got dressed and came out onto the Winfield's wooden deck.

Todd took one look at Chris's weird swimsuit and his glaring white legs and decided it might be time to ditch him and his bratty sister. *Maybe they don't really have summer on the East Coast,* he thought to himself. He led the gang back over the bridge and up the hill to Pioneer Park.

"The pool's up there," he said, pointing. "We'll see ya later. There's a place I want to show Jill."

Todd grabbed Jill's hand and led her in the opposite direction across the flat grassy space toward the creek that ran across the back of the park.

"Where we going?"

"You'll see." He wanted to get her away from Chris and Nancy so they wouldn't bug him.

"This park is beautiful. We don't have anything like it in Millersburg. You're so lucky to live here."

Todd shrugged. He didn't feel particularly lucky. And he didn't think Nevada City all that great. Besides, he had never known anything else.

"You guys flying out on Monday?"

"Uh huh," she answered simply.

"Looking forward to getting back?"

"Kind of." Jill felt the color red creeping up her neck. Why did she feel so nervous?

"I'll miss ya."

"Oh, really?" What else could she say? She didn't dare admit that she would miss him too, or that she thought she liked him.

"If you want, you can write me." Todd didn't know how else to say it. He thought he liked this . . . kid. Maybe he was pushing her too much, but he had to somehow let her know.

"Maybe," Jill said nervously. "Let's go swimming." She grabbed his hand and pulled him to follow her in the direction of the pool. She felt too nervous to continue the conversation anymore.

Later, as she lay on the hot concrete skirting surrounding the pool and watched Chris in his funny swimsuit, she thought how much she'd like to come back here. The dark blue sky, the smell of the pine trees, and the clear air all told her that somehow, someday, she'd come back here. And maybe she would write to Todd after all.

THE END

Turn to page 143.

Chris took charge. He knew they would have to do something to save Todd's life.

"Jill, will you stay here with him?" He saw her nod in the dim light. "He'll need someone to talk to and to keep a light on for him." Todd's flashlight had sunk under the water. Jill's flashlight was already noticeably dimmer. At least Todd could keep hearing her voice.

"Nancy and I will find our way back to the surface and get help."

As he turned back up the tunnel, Chris only hoped that Todd could hold on. He had never been very good at treading water himself and knew how tiring it could be. He prayed softly that God would help Todd and Jill. He asked God to help him make the right choices, too.

Nancy interrupted his thoughts. "Why are you mumbling like that?"

"I was praying, Nancy," he said softly.

She said, "Oh, does that really help?"

"Yeah, it does."

It didn't take them long to reach the candy bar intersection again.

"Which way now?" Nancy asked.

"We have two choices. We can either go take the Hershey's tunnel or the Nestlé Crunch tunnel. What do you think?"

"I think we should go down the Hershey's tunnel," Nancy said. "It just looks right to me."

But Chris felt the Nestlé Crunch tunnel looked right to him.

CHOICE ➤

If they take the Hershey's tunnel, turn to page 48.

If they take the Nestlé Crunch tunnel, turn to page 93.

"Look," said Todd to Chris and Nancy. "You two go ahead and explore the mine, but I'm going to take Jill swimming. You know how to get back to my house. Just be careful."

"OK," Chris said. He looked unhappy as he started walking back down the hill with his sister toward Nevada City and the mine.

As Chris and Nancy disappeared, Jill felt uneasy. "What happens if they get lost?" she asked Todd. "You'll still get blamed because you showed them where the mine opening was."

Todd knew Jill had a point. He did feel guilty. But he really did want to be with Jill, not Chris and Nancy. And this sure seemed like a good opportunity to get them out of the way. But as they stood there, neither of them made any attempt to go get their swimsuits on.

Finally, Jill couldn't stand it anymore. "Let's go after them. We can't let them go in there all by themselves and get lost. I really think they *need* you to protect them."

"OK, if that's what you want."

So they walked back down the hill through downtown Nevada City and over to the mine. There they found Chris and Nancy sitting at the mine entrance.

"You guys came!" Chris said. "I'm so glad you did. I

was afraid to take Nancy in there by myself. I was afraid I'd get her lost."

CHOICE

Turn to page 95.

Nancy continued to jump up and down, crying about the pain. Todd felt she was acting like a baby.

Chris hurt for his sister. He suggested she scoop up some of the cold river water to put on her lip until it felt better. But Nancy just kept dancing around.

After about twenty minutes, Nancy was still whimpering, and Todd decided he would have to call his mom or brother to pick them up early. Annoyed, he took Jill up to the pay phone located near the bridge and made the call.

"She'll be here in about forty minutes," he said after stepping out of the telephone booth. "Too bad Nancy's such a baby. She's ruining the day for everyone else."

Jill got defensive. "Have you thought that the sting might be hurting badly? Maybe she's a lot more sensitive to pain than you are."

Todd found it difficult to have any sympathy for Nancy. He always hated being around younger kids who couldn't control their crying when they got hurt.

"Maybe, but I've been stung by meat bees before, and it didn't affect me like that."

Chris and Nancy came up to meet the car when Todd's mom arrived. By now Nancy's face had swollen a little, and Mrs. Winfield noticed. The others had missed it because it had happened so gradually. Mrs. Winfield decided to drive them to the emergency room at Nevada County Hospital, just in case it was an allergic reaction to the sting. A few phone calls got them in touch with Chris and Nancy's mom so they could treat Nancy.

"It's just a mild reaction, but it's good that you brought her in," the emergency room doctor told Todd's mom. "Some allergic reactions to bee stings can have some pretty serious complications."

Todd felt guilty when he realized how serious the sting could have been. He hadn't thought that it could be anything but just painful.

Nancy felt much better after the doctor had injected her with the proper drug. But the gang's search for gold would have to wait until she was fully recovered in a few days. That was OK with Todd, but Chris had gold fever. *His* recovery wouldn't start until they launched a serious exploration of Todd's abandoned gold mine.

THE END

Turn to page 1 and help Chris get over his gold fever by making different choices along the way.

Or, turn to page 143.

"**G**ood idea," said Todd. He pulled his hand out of the pocket and manipulated the knife up toward the top. Finally it came out.

"I got it!" Todd said with satisfaction. "Now how are we gonna get the blade pulled out?" He made several attempts to get the blade out but ended up frustrated each time.

"I know," said Chris. "Let's put it in my mouth. I'll hold it with my teeth, and you can pull the blade out." Chris wasn't sure this would work, but it was worth a try.

Todd spent several minutes wriggling his body so that he could get the knife to Chris's mouth. When he finally had it, Todd worked at pulling on the blades. He told himself he'd never chew his fingernails again. Finally, "Got it!"

Todd cut one of the ropes around Chris's hands, and in a moment he was free. He then freed Todd. They stood up, looking around uncertainly.

"But where are we?" Chris asked.

"I don't know. I guess we'll just have to wander around and hope we find a way out."

"Yeah, and let's try not to run into those thieves again. I don't like the idea of getting shot."

They wandered for some time before they saw a light ahead.

"That looks like the lantern the thieves were using," Chris whispered. "I think we're back where we started."

Todd realized they had to be careful. He didn't want to get captured again. He thought he could find his way back to Scotty's backyard, so he led Chris away from the light and toward the way they came in. Finally, they saw the rope.

They ran to it and climbed up into Scotty's backyard, then ran to his house. Nobody was home. They couldn't believe it! Where had Scotty gone?

They managed to climb through Scotty's open window and called the police.

"I wanna report a . . . a . . . robbery," Todd stammered. "At the Gold Exchange." In a moment, a Lieutenant Grabowski came on the line.

"Calm down, son. Are you Chris Martin?"

"No, that's my friend. I'm Todd Winfield."

"I've got the two boys," he heard Grabowski call out to someone in the background. "Where are you now, son?"

"At Scotty Davidson's house on Richardson Avenue."

The two boys soon found out that Scotty and his mother had already contacted the police, and they had arrested three men for the attempted robbery from the vault at the Gold Exchange. But despite repeated questioning, the men wouldn't reveal where they'd left the boys. So everyone had been holding their breath, concerned for Chris and Todd's safety.

Everything that happened after the thieves were arrested seemed dull by comparison. Todd decided he

84

would never try to play the hero again. Nearly getting
killed will do that to you.

THE END
Turn to page 143.

Todd was just about to ask Nevada another question when Jill reached out to pull on his arm.

"Come on, Todd. Let's get out of here," she said in a low voice.

He glanced at her face, and the concerned look he saw convinced him to do as she asked. With a sigh he turned and headed back up the trail.

The four made their way back toward the beach in silence until they passed the two men using the dredge.

"Why did that man shoot at us?" Nancy asked.

"I told ya. These miners are a weird breed. They're afraid the whole world is trying to steal their pokes."

"But I was only playing with the shovel."

"Yeah, but as far as he was concerned you were messing with his way of life. He uses that shovel and sluice like other people use a machine. That's just about all that guy's got."

"Well, he didn't have to shoot at us," said Jill. "He could have hurt somebody."

Todd shook his head. "Believe me, he knew exactly what he was doing. Just scaring off a bunch of *punk kids*." Nancy smiled at him, which made him feel good inside. He knew he had to get everyone home—and in one piece—by five o'clock. If they all stayed together, they

86

might actually make it. But it was sure a long ride back up
that hill!

THE END

Turn to page 143.

"Todd, I'm sorry. I'd love to show your friends the vault, but . . . I'm afraid I can't do that. I'd be asking for trouble if I showed it to everyone who might be interested. I hope you understand."

Todd had been afraid of that. "Sure," he said. But he found it difficult to hide the disappointment he felt at not being able to deliver on his promise.

"Come on," said Chris, "let's go explore the Holbrooke lobby."

The four kids headed for the lobby, where they raided the soft drink machine. As they sat down with their drinks, Todd came up with another idea. "I know! Let's go over to the local AM/FM radio station, and you can watch the disk jockeys through the window."

Everyone thought that sounded like a good idea, except Chris who felt a little shortchanged. Watching a disk jockey was hardly his idea of a fair trade for exploring a gold mine or a vault full of gold.

At the radio station, they sat in front of the plate glass window and watched the AM announcer, "Wonderful Walt," do his afternoon talk show.

"OK, all of you out there in radio land, our next guest is Mr. Graham Robertson, an expert on Nevada County history and author of *49er Gold*. Tell us Mr. Robertson, what has made Grass Valley so colorful over the years?"

The bearded historian spoke slowly. "Well, Walt, as you know, Grass Valley and its sister, Nevada City, are known today for their beautiful Sierra environment. But in the last century, the area was set apart from others because of the gold."

Chris leaned forward in his chair.

"When you look at all the old photographs of the city," Robertson continued, "during the heyday of the mining operations, you'll see that the hills looked pretty desolate. Most of the trees had been cut down to provide fuel for huge steam engines that kept the mines pumped dry."

"So people didn't come here for the beauty back then?"

"No, it was the gold, plain and simple."

Chris licked his lips.

"You know," added Wonderful Walt, "I've lived here long enough to remember when that short freeway between Grass Valley and Nevada City was put in. They had to fence off the construction site because people kept looking for gold each night when the crews shut down the project."

"Yes," added Robertson, "and the company that did the pavement bought and crushed mine tailings for the gravel they used, and they paid for the gravel with all the gold they processed out of it."

Chris turned to Todd. "Does that mean there's gold all around here?"

Todd nodded. "Yeah." Chris sure had gold fever.

"Maybe we should go on one of those mine tours after all, so you could see for yourself how they ran the mines."

Turn to page 61.

Jill seemed to be panicking. But Todd knew he couldn't go down there. He looked down the roadway, where the curve turned back to make an S, and noticed that the bank's slope was much more gradual at that point.

"Stay right here so you can tell me where he is," he told Jill. Then he ran downhill and jumped over the side. As Todd picked up speed, gravel and dirt clouded up at his feet and raced him down the slope. Finally he reached what appeared to be a deer trail cutting sideways back toward where Chris must be.

He followed the path, occasionally looking up at Jill to get his bearing until he came to the tangled bushes. Because of the denseness of the thicket, it took a few moments to spot Chris, who lay sprawled in the middle of the small hardwood trees. Fortunately for Chris, the manzanita was green and pliable and had not yet grown brittle with age.

"Chris. Can you hear me?"

Todd thought he heard something, maybe some groaning. He desperately wanted to see some sign of life. He pushed his way into the undergrowth, and when he reached Chris, his eyes opened.

"Where am I?"

"You flew off that road," Todd said, pointing over his head, "back up there."

Chris took one look up and closed his eyes again. "No wonder I hurt."

Todd had heard stories about how it wasn't good to move somebody who had been in an accident; you could hurt them more, especially if their back had been injured.

"Can you move?"

Chris opened his eyes again and smiled. "I think so." He managed to sit up, then with Todd's help he stood. "So far, so good. I don't think I broke anything," Chris said, moving his arms and legs gingerly. The two guys worked their way back out of the manzanita.

"Man, are you lucky!" Todd exclaimed. "See how far up you were?"

Chris looked up again, then shook his head in amazement. "I guess God protected me."

"You can say that again. Let's get back up to the road."

It took the two guys about ten minutes to follow the deer path and then struggle up the bank where Todd had come down. By the time they reached Jill, Chris felt pretty good.

"I'm so glad you're all right," she said. "I was worried sick waiting for you guys." Except for a few rips in his trunks and shirt and a few scrapes, Jill noticed that Chris didn't look bad at all. Not what she had expected, to say the least.

"Hey, man, you know you did two somersaults in the air?" Todd felt he had to lighten things up. "I'll bet when all the animals down there saw those flashy shorts spinning through the air and coming their way, they hightailed it out of the territory."

Chris and Jill both laughed. Chris guessed he must have looked really weird flying through the air like that.

Todd straightened the wheel on his brother's bike, and he reminded Chris this bike had hand brakes. They continued down the road, this time much slower. When they reached the bridge, Nancy sat waiting.

"What took you guys so long? I've never been around such *slow* people before." Then she took one look at her brother and said, "Don't tell me. I don't want to know."

CHOICE

Turn to page 37.

Chris just knew he had to be right this time—the Nestlé Crunch tunnel had to be the right one. They must get out quickly for Todd's sake. Chris and Nancy walked for quite some time before coming to another intersection.

"This is it! Look, there's the mine car."

It didn't take them long to follow the string back out to the crawl shaft and out to the sunshine beyond. As soon as they came out, Chris knew he had to get help in a hurry.

He found a telephone booth across the street from the old brewery and called the fire department.

"You say your friend has fallen into a dip pit filled with water, in one of the abandoned mines? Stay right where you're at. We'll be there in just a second."

Zong! Zong! Zong!

They heard an alarm go off through the city. Only two minutes later, a jeep charged over the bridge, and a moment later a car raced by, both obviously responding to the alarm.

Chris felt awful. All this wouldn't be happening if he hadn't insisted upon going into the mine in the first place. In a moment the rescue truck arrived at their location.

Inside the mine, Jill did what she could to keep Todd's spirits up. "Todd, are you OK?"

"Yeah. . . . Legs are getting tired . . . gonna try . . . to float . . . for awhile."

"OK. Don't try to talk. I know it's hard for you."

Todd seemed very tired, and Jill knew if he couldn't swim anymore, he might drown. She couldn't stand the thought of watching that happen right in front of her eyes.

O Lord, Jill began to pray, *I haven't been talking to you much lately, but Todd needs your help. Please, Lord, let help come before he gets too tired or cold.*

"Umsp." She heard Todd gasp for air.

"What's wrong?"

"Can't . . . float. . . . Keep going . . . under."

Jill continued to pray frantically under her breath. "O God, please make them hurry."

The fireman looked straight into Chris's eyes. "Tell us again exactly where they are."

Chris explained the route they had taken and where he thought Todd and Jill were located. He told them about all the markers they had used to get out, while the fireman quickly set up their underground gear: helmets with headlights, ropes, stretcher, blankets, and first-aid kits.

While he described how to get there, Chris overheard one of the firemen use the word *hypothermia*. He had thought about what effects the cold water might have on Todd's body.

In a moment the crew entered the shaft and disappeared. Chris and Nancy could only sit and wait. Chris was overcome with grief.

Turn to page 35.

"**W**ell, I *could* let you guys go in alone," said Todd. "But then what would you do if you ran into a swamp creature or something? I think you'll need my protection."

"Swamp creature?" Nancy asked.

"I know *you* could handle it, Nancy. It's your brother who wouldn't stand a chance." Nancy giggled and smiled at Chris. Chris poked her. "Come on," said Todd.

They entered the tunnel, and Todd led them back in with his flashlight pointing the way. Soon they reached the place where they had found the underground tracks.

"Which way do you think?" Chris asked. He wanted desperately to find something so he could prove to the other Ringers that he'd really had his adventure. If they happened to find some gold, that would be even better—but he didn't really expect anything that good.

"Well, the tracks seem to be going downhill this way." Todd pointed to their left. "My guess is that we'll be more likely to find something of value if we go up the grade maybe toward the original mouth of the mine."

"But wouldn't the gold be that way?" Nancy asked, using her small flashlight beam as a pointer.

Todd asked himself silently how he had managed to get himself into this stupid mess. *This kid really needs a muzzle,* he thought.

"Do you have any idea how deep these mine shafts

are? They go for miles and miles straight down. And all you'll find if you go deep enough is water. When they stopped mining they stopped pumping out all the water, and many of the shafts filled back up to the original water level."

"OK, so let's go right." Chris started to lead the way, stepping past Todd. "Nancy, tie that string to something and start rolling it out as we go."

"OK," she said, but Todd wondered if she would get it right. It would be just their luck that she'd get them all lost.

They walked for a long time, passing several small shafts just like the one they had come out of, and then they came to a four-way tunnel intersection. The tracks crossed and went in all four directions.

"Now which way?" Jill shivered against Todd's arm. "I'm afraid we're going to get completely lost. This place is too scary." Now she wished she had never heard of gold mines. She really just wanted to go back.

"Look! There's a mine car!" Nancy ran over to an ore cart that was off the tracks. She stuck her head inside. "And look, there's gold in here!" She held up a rock.

They all came over and aimed their flashlights at the rocks in the bed of the car. Everyone examined a different rock.

"Sure doesn't look like gold," Jill said.

"If there's any gold in these rocks, we probably wouldn't see it anyway," Todd remarked. "That's why they had those big stamping machines, remember? They had to crush the rock and then break it down to find the ore.

Besides, it's more likely that this is just rock that was being removed to lengthen one of the shafts."

"Look! I've struck it rich! Look at that shiny spot!" Nancy held up a heavy rock, and everyone could clearly see that one spot did actually shine. "Let's take it! I'll bet it's real gold!"

"Yes," said Jill. "Let's take it out. Now we can go back and see if it's worth anything."

"Let's not leave yet. We've just started to explore. Suppose there's a whole lot of ore up ahead." Chris didn't know what was up ahead, but he wanted to find out.

CHOICE ⇒

If the group goes back with the rock, turn to page 67.

If the group continues on, turn to page 128.

"This just isn't gonna work," said Todd. "I can't get it. My fingers are aching."

"There must be something we can do," Chris said.

For a long time the two of them just sat there wondering if they would ever see the light of day again. Then Chris got another idea.

"Why don't I try to untie your rope with my teeth?"

Todd laughed. "Your teeth, huh?" Todd shrugged. He really didn't think Chris's teeth would be any match for the tight ropes digging into his wrists, but at this point anything was worth trying. After what seemed like an hour of trying, Chris finally gave up. Both boys fell asleep from exhaustion.

Todd woke up later when he heard a noise. Not knowing who it might be, he kept quiet.

"Chris? Todd?" someone called out. "Chris? Todd?"

"We're here! We're in here!" Todd called back, waking Chris by his shouts.

In a moment two rescuers had found them.

"Oh, it's good to see you two. We were afraid the thieves had shot you."

"You know about the thieves?" Chris asked.

"Yeah. They left half of the gold behind, but they got away before we could arrest them. Your friend Scotty tipped us off, but we were too late to catch them."

Later, Todd and Chris had to file a report with the police. Lieutenant Grabowski wanted to know anything they could tell him about the suspects.

"The man who seemed to be in charge used to work at Mickey's Hamburgers on Main Street."

"You sure?"

"I'm positive. If I saw his picture, I could identify him."

Before long the police identified the suspect as a man named Andy Grayson. They said it would only be a matter of time before they brought the fugitives to justice. "Gold tends to attract attention."

As Chris well knew. At this point though, he and Todd both were just glad to be alive.

THE END

Turn to page 143.

Chris and Nancy started up the Nestlé Crunch tunnel, hoping it would lead them back the way they came. They walked for a long time before they came to another intersection.

"The car! Look, the car!" Nancy couldn't believe how much she had wanted to get back to this point. "And there's the ball of string. Now we can get out of here."

They followed the string back to the smaller shaft and then out to daylight. By now Chris knew it must already be close to four in the afternoon. He had to get someone to help him find the others.

Back in the tunnel, Todd and Jill began to listen to their stomachs groan.

"You have anything left to eat?" Jill asked. "I've eaten everything I brought with me."

Todd had been forcing himself not to eat anything. He had an apple and a box of raisins and a small package of peanuts. He offered everything to Jill but suggested she not eat the peanuts.

"They'll tend to make you thirsty, and you don't want to get thirsty if you can avoid it."

"Well, at least we can find a tunnel that has water in it if we get real thirsty." Jill didn't like the idea of drinking such water, but she knew if they got thirsty enough, it might be their only choice.

Todd didn't say anything. He had a very good reason for doing everything he could to keep himself or Jill from getting thirsty. He knew, but didn't tell Jill, that a lot of the water in the old mines had arsenic or some other poison in it. He gave her the apple knowing it had a lot of liquid in it.

They sat down and rested.

Back on the surface, Chris had a decision to make. Who could he tell that his friends were trapped underground? Perhaps he should call over to Todd's house and tell his parents. Then again, maybe he should just dial 911 and let the emergency people tell him what to do.

CHOICE ⇒

If he calls Todd's parents, turn to page 15.

If he calls 911, turn to page 122.

"**A**ll right, so you wanna explore the mine. But like I said, how ya gonna do it without a flashlight?" Todd said. He wasn't really worried about that, though. After all, he'd explored this shaft years ago. He knew it split into two separate dead ends. He just wouldn't tell them about any of the openings that led into the really deep and dangerous mines.

"We could make a torch," Nancy offered.

Chris sniffed and thought, *She always has something dumb to say.*

"And look, here it is!" She picked up a discarded newspaper lying on the ground and rolled it up into a tight cylinder shape.

"But you don't have anything to light it with," Jill reminded.

A smile formed on Chris's mouth. "I helped burn the trash this morning and . . . I still have all these with me." He held up a box of wooden matches.

It didn't take long for Chris to light the torch, and they all entered the tunnel. He led the way followed by Nancy, Todd, and then Jill. Todd had to take Jill's hand to coax her into the tunnel.

After they had gone about thirty feet into the cold hillside, the tunnel split into a T.

"Which way should we go, Todd?"

"Doesn't make any difference. Both are dead ends."

Chris turned to the left and followed the curving shaft until it came to a wide space that ended suddenly in a small chamber. By the flickering light of the makeshift torch they could see that newspapers, old clothes, and a few empty dry cereal boxes covered the floor.

"Looks like somebody lived here," said Chris.

"This place gives me the creeps," Jill said. She shivered against Todd's arm. It felt like the temperature had dropped about thirty degrees from outside. "Let's get out of here."

"Ouch!" The torch had burned down to Chris's fingers, and he let it drop to the floor. In just a moment it flickered out, plunging the group into darkness.

The girls each let out muffled screams, then Nancy started giggling. "This is fun. Just like in the movies."

"Can you find the matches?"

Chris reached into his jeans pocket and found the crushed box containing the matches. He fumbled with it for a moment in the darkness, trying to open it by feel, when it suddenly popped out of his hands scattering the wooden matchsticks all over the floor.

"Oh, great! You dropped them?" Jill was not a happy miner.

"It's OK, I'll find 'em." Chris bent down and began to feel for the sticks. No telling what he might find on the damp floor of the chamber. Three match sticks, but still no box.

"Well, the tunnel isn't that long," Todd offered. "We can always feel our way back to the opening. Already his eyes seemed to be adjusting to the small amount of light coming from where they had turned left.

"I've got it," Chris cried, finding the box. After several unsuccessful attempts, he managed to strike one of the sticks against the striking strip on the side of the box and the head burst into flame.

"Good, let's get out of here." Jill and Todd started to turn around.

"Wait you guys! I've found a lamp." In a moment, Chris managed to light the wick of a small kerosene lamp that hung from the ceiling of the chamber. The flickering light wasn't very bright, but they could clearly see the entire room.

Someone had certainly used the room as a place to sleep, or perhaps as a hideout or fort. An old chair with its stuffing half popped out rested against the wall, where a large dark square could barely be seen. Chris moved the lamp from its hook, and as he did, all the shadows moved with him. He realized the dark square must be another tunnel—smaller and close to the floor.

"Look at this. I thought you said this tunnel was a dead end."

Todd had never seen an opening when he had visited this chamber in past years. But that had been a long time ago. He bent down to look into the hole with the help of the lantern.

"Never seen this before."

"This place is spooky. For all we know, some homeless bum lives here. Let's go before he comes back.

Let's go swimming—it's a lot safer and more fun." Jill just didn't want to be here anymore.

"We just can't leave without checking out this tunnel," Chris said.

CHOICE ⇒

If the group goes swimming, turn to page 19.

If they go in, turn to page 31.

"**W**ho could possibly be down here?" Jill asked, her voice barely above a whisper.

"Could just be some other kids," Scotty suggested.

"Or maybe someone doing work for the city." Chris didn't think it had to be a problem.

"I doubt that," said Todd. "But I'm sure curious."

"Let's just get out of here," said Jill with a little shake in her voice. "We'll probably get in trouble for being down here."

"Why don't you girls wait here with Chris and Scotty, and I'll go a little farther to see what's happening," said Todd.

"No way. If you go—I go," said Chris. "I'm not missing out on the action."

"But Chris, the girls don't have any light without you. You need to stay here with them."

"You're not leaving me here," whispered Jill.

"Me, neither," Nancy spoke up, almost too loudly.

"OK. But you all have to be quiet. We don't know who's up there in the tunnel. We may find ourselves in big trouble if they find out we're down here."

The five of them moved slowly behind Scotty's guidance. The closer they got, the clearer the sounds became. Someone was digging. The kids could also see some light coming from a Coleman lantern hanging from a wooden beam.

"How much longer, you think?" spoke a gruff male voice up ahead.

"We could break through in twenty minutes," said another male voice.

"OK, let me call Wilson. Don't want any screwups; we're just too close to blow it now."

Suddenly, a man appeared in the main tunnel, in plain view of the five kids. He picked up a radio and took it with him as he joined the other guy.

"Ground Hog to Eagle, do you read me?"

Squalk. "Ground Hog, this is Eagle. I read you." Todd could barely hear the man on the radio.

"Ground hog is in place, ready to surface. How's our activity level?"

"Still negative, Ground Hog. Negative."

"OK, meet you for dinner in fifteen minutes."

Todd made everyone back up out of sight. He sensed the men getting ready to come out from where they had been digging. In a moment they went off down a different tunnel and disappeared.

"Are they gone?" Chris whispered.

"I think so."

"Let's go look at what they were doing," said Scotty.

"But what if they come back and catch us?" Jill didn't like this at all.

"Let's wait a few more minutes," Todd cautioned.

When at last they crept up to the place where the men had been, the kids found that they had dug a fresh new hole off to one side up toward the surface. An assortment of digging tools, the two-way radio, and several crowbars and cutting torches sat in a pile. From the looks of all the fast-food wrappers, it seemed obvious they had been here for some time.

"What's all this about?" Jill asked.

Todd didn't know. "Where are we, anyway?"

Scotty looked up and down the tunnel for a moment. "Somewhere under East Main Street. Hard to tell for sure."

"Why do you think they're digging? Are they looking for gold?" asked Nancy.

"No. There wouldn't be any gold up that way, toward the surface. Maybe they're just trying to open a storm drain or something for the city."

Todd shook his head. "Then why the mysterious two-way radio talk? No, I think these guys are up to something."

"Let's just get out of here before they come back and we get in trouble." Jill wanted to be gone—the sooner, the better.

Turn to page 130.

"You think she'll be all right?" Jill asked.

"Yeah. I don't know all that much you can do for it anyway, except putting something cold on it. She'll be all right." Todd just hoped she wouldn't act like a baby.

After a few minutes, Nancy did settle down, but she wouldn't smile and didn't want to eat any more. "Will someone go in the water with me? It's no fun swimming by yourself."

"Sure," said Chris, getting up.

As they walked to the edge of the cold river, Todd glanced at Jill. He had to admit that she looked kind of attractive with her long brown hair and yellow bathing suit.

"So you're in seventh grade?"

"Uh huh." She wondered if he was trying to put her down because of her age.

Jill's one-word answer didn't provide much room for Todd to make conversation. Talking to girls had never been his specialty.

"Did you want me to show you my special swimming hole?" Todd asked. The words, though out of his own mouth, had come from another universe, a universe of Things to Say if You Want to Sound Dorky, a universe not under his control. Todd felt the embarrassment wash over his face.

110

"Sure," Jill said. "Why not?" She felt warmed by Todd's question; it sounded like he wanted to be around her.

"Come on," he said as he led Jill down a river path. When they had climbed a small hill and rounded a bend in the river, he stopped and pointed down at the water. "That's it."

Jill peered over the side at a small blue pool next to the raging white water of the river. It did look inviting under the hot day's sun.

"How do you get down there?"

"You just jump."

"Jump? It must be twelve feet to the water!"

CHOICE ➤

If Jill jumps, turn to page 137.

If Jill won't jump, turn to page 7.

"Look," Todd said, "why don't you all sit here for a second and I'll go up the right shaft and check it out. You should still be able to hear me. Either way, I'll come back, and we'll find the way back to the candy bar wrappers."

Jill wanted to go with him so they started up the right-hand tunnel together. It didn't take them long to come back to the candy bar intersection.

"Good. At least we found our way back here. Now let's get Chris and Nancy."

In a few moments all of them were back at the same intersection. Nancy picked up her "gold" rock and stopped sniveling.

"Let's try the Nestlé Crunch bar tunnel this time. I'm sure that's the way we came."

"Chris, isn't that what you said about the Hershey's tunnel?" Jill felt frustrated.

They walked down the Nestlé Crunch bar tunnel for quite some time, careful not to take any shaft that went off at an angle, hoping to get back to the intersection where the mine car had been left.

"I think we've come too far. This just doesn't seem like the same tunnel." Nancy couldn't help feeling that they were going around in circles.

"We've got to go further until we're sure that we're not in the right tunnel. If we turn around too soon, and this is

112

the right tunnel, we'll never want to try this one again, and we'll never—" Todd stopped himself from continuing. No sense in making the situation any worse than it already was.

"Look! The mine car!" Nancy ran ahead and started talking so loudly that the echo noise hurt the others' ears. "And look! There's the ball of string leading back up from the way we came!"

They all felt relieved. Now they definitely could get out without much of a problem. By now, even Chris wanted to go out. He had had enough adventure for one day.

"Let's take Nancy's rock to the Wells Fargo assay office," Chris said. It was the perfect excuse to get out. And he had to admit, he was getting anxious to find out if they had really found some gold.

"That old office is just a museum now," said Todd. "But there is a place over in Grass Valley, the Gold Exchange, where you can have it analyzed."

"I don't want to go there. I want to go swimming." Jill seemed afraid that she would never get a chance to get wet.

CHOICE ➡️

If they go swimming, turn to page 73.

If they go to the Gold Exchange, turn to page 67.

Just then a vehicle came up the highway. The driver slowed, and when he saw the bicycle on the ground and Todd waving at him, he stopped his pickup on the side of the road. He got out and walked over to Todd and Jill.

"What happened?"

"My friend crashed his bicycle and flew way down there."

"Oh my," said the man peering down the hill. "Awful steep down there." He turned toward his truck. "Let's use my winch."

The man walked back to his truck and hooked a rope to the winch he had on the front of his pickup truck. He and Todd worked up a harness, then Todd slipped it on. He went to the edge, carefully stepped off, and made a slow descent toward Chris, using the rope to keep him from losing his footing as he went down.

Todd reached a deer path, then pushed his way into the manzanita undergrowth where Chris had landed. Relief surged through Todd when he saw Chris stir.

"You all right?" Todd asked, kneeling beside him.

"I don't know. I feel like I just died."

Todd shook his head. "Heaven would have rejected you in those trunks." They both laughed. Chris was dazed, but otherwise he seemed OK.

"Where am I?" said Chris, sitting up.

"You flew off the road, up there." Todd pointed up over his head."

"No kidding." As Chris looked all the way up to the road he couldn't believe he had fallen that far. And he didn't even remember the fall.

Chris stood up slowly. "I'm all right." They worked their way back out of the manzanita to a deer trail above it.

"Look," Todd said, "I've got a rope to help you walk back up the hill. If I put this harness around you, you think you can make it back up there?"

"Sure." Chris felt a lot better now that his head had cleared. It didn't take long for him to work his way back up the hill, as the winch pulled him gently upwards. Once he reached the road, they threw the line down for Todd and they winched him up, too.

"I'm so glad you're OK," Jill said to Chris. "I prayed that you would be."

"Well, your prayers sure worked," Chris said. Except for a few rips in his trunks and shirt and a few scrapes, he didn't look bad at all.

When the man in the truck realized that Chris hadn't been injured, he got ready to leave. The group thanked him for all his help, and he drove off.

Todd straightened the wheel on his brother's bike and reminded Chris the bike had hand brakes. Then the three of them continued down the road, this time going much slower. When they reached the bridge, Nancy sat waiting.

"What took you guys so long? I've never been around such *slow* people before." She took one look at her brother and just shook her head.

115

Turn to page 37.

Turn to page 37.

The girls prevailed, and they climbed back up the rope ladder into Scotty's backyard.

"Let me ask my mom if she'll take us swimming," he said.

Mrs. Davidson agreed to take the kids back to Todd's house to get their swimsuits and then over to the Grass Valley pool. Chris noticed that Scotty seemed to be paying a lot of attention to his kid sister. He found that difficult to understand.

At the pool, Jill put her towel down on the deck. Todd sat down beside her.

"How do you like high school?" she asked.

"Beats junior high, I can tell ya that," Todd answered. "They treat you more like a grown-up. This'll be my sophomore year."

Todd wished Jill didn't live so far away. He could get to like her if she lived somewhere close. But Washington, D.C., seemed like halfway around the world.

"Do you have a girlfriend?" Jill asked.

Todd thought for a moment before answering. "Kinda," he lied. "Used to spend a lot of time with a girl named Margie Blackwood. But haven't seen her since summer vacation started."

"Oh."

"What about you? Got a boyfriend?"

"No. My folks say I'm too young. And when I start dating, they only want me to date Christian boys."

That seemed unusual to Todd. "They real religious?"

"No, silly. Being a Christian isn't being *religious.* It just means you live your life for Jesus instead of living for yourself."

Todd had never heard anyone talk like that before. A lot of his friends went to church, but none of them really talked about God or anything like that. It was just something they did on Sunday, like watching TV.

"I don't go to church. Seems a waste of time to me."

Jill nodded. She knew lots of kids who felt that way. But she knew church only made sense when you had given your life to Jesus. "I don't go to church because my parents want me to," she said quietly. "I go because I want to. Now that I know the Lord, it's kind of neat to learn about him and sing and be with other Christian kids."

"Oh." Todd didn't know what else to say.

"The guys have a gang at their church called the Ringers," Jill continued. "It's not an official gang with rules and jackets and all that. But we hang around a lot. Of course, I'll have to go back home when school starts, so I'll probably miss a lot of adventures."

A gang? Todd thought. The gangs he heard about sure didn't go to church.

"Ringer means someone who acts like someone else, and since we're supposed to act like Christ, we're Ringers. It helps to have Christian friends who support you, because not everyone at school is a Christian and sometimes you feel like an outsider." Suddenly Jill stopped herself, sensing Todd's uneasiness.

"Sounds interesting," he said, but he seemed lost in thought. Neither of them spoke for several minutes. Todd liked Jill, and now he knew why. She was different. Her faith wasn't some fakey thing that she used when it was convenient. She was actually enthusiastic about Jesus—like God was a *person,* not a force in the sky. Todd guessed her faith made her what she was—and he found himself wanting the kind of enthusiasm she had. But another side of him was afraid of "getting religious."

Jill didn't know what to make of Todd's silence, so she figured she'd better drop the subject. Maybe she could explain herself better if she wrote him after they went home. "After we go home next week, would you write to me if I wrote to you?"

"Sure." Todd would write to her if she sent him a letter. Who knew what might come of it?

After several hours, the five kids called Mrs. Davidson to pick them up.

Jill's conversation with Todd about Jesus had caused her to think about her own life. Just talking about how she felt about the Lord made her realize how important he really was to her—and that to some people he wasn't important at all. She wished she could make Todd change his mind. She would soon learn that she had already started to.

THE END

Turn to page 143.

Todd led the small group farther down the river. He had never been down here before, but he had heard there were miners who worked this part of the Yuba. He had no idea what they'd find.

"Look!" Nancy ran over to a large wooden box sitting up on the bank. There was a shovel leaning against it. "A sluice box of our own! Somebody must have thrown it away."

Even though the box looked like it might fall apart, the moment Todd saw the shovel, he knew that the owner had to be nearby. Nancy started to scoop up a shovel full of sand to put into the box.

"Don't, Nancy. Leave it alone." But his words were interrupted by a loud noise.

Zang!

Todd immediately fell down between two boulders. Everyone else remained standing.

"Get down! Get down, you guys! Somebody's shooting at us."

Everyone dove for cover but Nancy. She twisted her skinny body one way, then another, trying to see who could have shot at them.

Zang! When the second shot ricocheted off a rock, Nancy shrieked and sprawled down between two rocks just like the others.

"See what I mean?" Todd stuck his head up just enough to try to see who had fired at them. In a moment a grizzled old man with unkempt hair the color of mud on vines came out of the trees and walked down toward the river.

"Who you think ya are, huh? Just a buncha dumb punk kids." The man looked angry. There was a dark gap where two of his front teeth had once been.

"We didn't mean anything, mis-ter." Chris's voice cracked.

"How'd I know ya ain't plannin' ta rip off my diggins, huh? Couple a' punk kids liable to lead the whole world down here."

"We aren't punks. Punks have colored hair," said Nancy. The man swung his rifle in her direction and glared. Nancy screamed and clutched at Chris.

"Nancy!" he hissed under his breath. "Keep quiet!"

"Nevada?" Todd thought he recognized the guy.

The man brought the barrel of his rifle over and faced it toward Todd. "How you know ma name, kid?"

Looking straight down that rifle bore made Todd's head spin. "You're kinda famous around here. Almost everybody knows about Nevada."

"Famous, huh? What kind of slop you trying to sling at me kid?"

Todd gulped. If that rifle went off, he was history. "I've heard about you. You're the only miner left who dates back to the hard-rock days."

Nevada eased his rifle back toward his body. "Well,

yer all lucky I'm in a good mood, or you'd all be bear bait by now. Nobody messes with my diggings. Understand?"

Chris nodded and backed up, only to stumble over a rock and fall on his back in the sand.

"What's yer problem kid? Who dresses ya anyway?" he finished with a toothless grin. He obviously considered Chris's trunks as weird-looking as Todd did. Especially now, with the rips from Chris's three-point landing in the manzanita bushes.

Jill helped Chris up, and everyone but Todd started backing up, turning up river toward the trail they had come down. But Todd realized Nevada might be an interesting character to talk to, especially because Chris really wanted to know more about gold mining.

CHOICE

If they go back up the river, turn to page 85.

If Todd tries to talk to Nevada, turn to page 9.

With shaking fingers, Chris dialed 911 on the pay telephone. When the operator came on the line, he immediately told her what had happened. Soon a team of volunteer firemen showed up and asked him to take them to the tunnel opening.

They took down all the instructions as to which way Todd and Jill had gone and then went into the mine armed with helmets with lights on them, backpacks, rope, and other rescue gear.

"Well, we've sat here for a long time," said Todd. "We'd probably better get moving."

They had eaten up the last of their food, and Todd feared that if he didn't keep Jill moving, she might totally give up. He knew they could be in this mine for days before they got rescued—*if* they got rescued. So, even though they felt tired, they started walking again.

Fortunately the firemen on the rescue squad knew that they were in the old Banner Mine and had maps of all the various intersections. They also made careful chalk markings every time they came to a new intersection so that they could keep track of their location.

"Do you hear that?" asked one of the firemen. "I thought I heard something."

"Help!" A cry came from off in the distance. "Help!" They heard it again.

"Up this way."

Jill had heard them before Todd did and had started calling for help. When the firemen finally came to the two, she burst into tears. Never again would she go into an abandoned mine!

Just as Todd had feared, his parents put him on restriction for the rest of the summer—not terminal grounding, but close to it. In a strange way, though, he felt glad. It was pretty stupid of him to let himself get talked into a situation like that in the first place. He had known how dangerous it would be to enter an abandoned mine shaft. Yet he listened to those who knew less.

He sighed to himself. "Brainless, Todd. Brainless."

But not—thanks to God's protection—fatal. And for the first time in his life, Todd was grateful he was going through a punishment. Hey, it beat the alternative.

THE END

Turn to page 143.

"**R**un for it," Todd whispered, and each kid took off in a different direction.

Todd kept expecting to hear gunshots, but the only thing he heard was the fast pounding of his own heartbeat as he escaped into the night. After a few moments he managed to find both Chris and Scotty.

"What do you think we should do now?" Scotty asked.

"We have to go to the police."

Todd knew they were right. They couldn't let the thieves make off with all that gold. So they quickly ran down to the Grass Valley Police Department.

"Let me get this straight," said the desk officer. "You guys were just exploring in a mine? And came across some people who dug up into the Holbrooke?" He didn't sound too convinced.

"We saw all the gold with our own eyes," Scotty said.

"You just happened to be exploring at four o'clock in the morning? Come on kids, why don't you just go back home and go to bed and leave me to do my job. You're lucky I don't feel like calling your parents."

Todd could see the officer would never believe them.

"Let's get outta here," he said, disgusted. "We'll just have to contact the County Sheriff, or maybe even the FBI."

"Wait!" Chris said, whirling around. "Here!" He held

up the gold Krugerrand he'd picked up at the mine exit. "The thieves dropped this."

The officer looked at the coin and then back to the kids and picked up the telephone.

"Lieutenant, I'm sorry to wake you up this time of the morning, but I have something I think you might want to check into."

Ten minutes later, when Lieutenant Grabowski arrived at the station, he decided to check into the kid's story. He called Jack Cookson, the owner of the Gold Exchange, and had him come down to his shop along with several deputies. He also went to the trapdoor behind Josie's. By now the sun was just starting to come up.

"Doesn't seem to be anyone here," he said.

The radio blared and the Lieutenant's men quickly confirmed that the Gold Exchange had been robbed—and the thieves had come in through the floor. They would be entering the tunnel at that end.

Unfortunately, even with Scotty's help, they could find no one in the mine. The men had obviously been alerted and had run, leaving half of the gold behind.

A reporter from a local radio station interviewed the three kids on the radio on Saturday. And a story about their adventures appeared in the *Grass Valley Union*. But no one knew where the thieves went with their loot.

Todd at least felt glad that they had saved some of the riches that had been deposited in the Gold Exchange vault.

THE END
Turn to page 143.

Chris didn't want to wait, but he didn't want to be a pain either, so he spread out his towel next to Todd's. "All right. Let's toast ourselves for awhile. But maybe you could tell me more about gold."

Todd really just wanted to sleep in the warm sunlight. But, he did have a true story he'd heard from his uncle, one he knew would probably get Chris all worked up.

"My uncle knows of a guy, a hard-rock miner, who was gonna buy the rights to one of the abandoned mines."

"Yeah?"

"Well, he went to the library where they've got all these microfilm copies of old newspaper issues of *The Union,* which tell all about the town and the mines. And he found that one of the mines, I don't remember which one, closed down after the owner died and his widow felt the foreman was cheatin' her. And this guy figured, 'Hey, they didn't finish the vein they were working. There's gotta be a lot of gold just waitin' to be dug out.' So he thought he'd buy the rights and reopen that mine. Only gonna cost him $150,000 for the rights."

Chris's eyeballs looked like saucers. "Really? That makes sense. Did he buy it?"

"Naw. He kept reading and discovered that after the foreman got fired, he hired on at a mine on the other side of the hill. And right after that, they changed the direction of some of their shafts."

"So what's that mean?"

Todd shook his head. Chris seemed so dense. "Don't you get it? They changed the direction of their shafts 'cause they cleaned out the first mine's vein from the other side of the hill."

Chris nodded. "So he never bought the mine?"

"Right."

The sun went dark and for a moment everyone thought a sudden storm had hit them.

"Hey! Stop that!" Jill cried.

Nancy shook her skinny head back and forth, sending water drops all over her three older companions until Chris chased her back to the river. "Come on in you guys, the water's greeeeaaat!" she called as she splashed back into the frigid water.

"OK," Chris said at last, "show me the gold in the river."

Turn to page 63.

"OK," Todd said slowly. "Let's go a little deeper."

"But which way?" Jill's stomach turned upside down every time they made the decision to go deeper.

"Let's go down this tunnel, the one that has the car in it. That way we'll know when we come back to this point." Everyone agreed with Chris and they started up that tunnel.

They walked for a long time and passed several side tunnels before they came to another four-way intersection of tunnels. When they stopped, Nancy began to complain.

"This rock is heavy. Will someone carry it for me?"

"Why are you still carrying that rock? You could have left it back there, and we could have picked it up on the way out."

"I didn't want to lose it."

"Nancy, where's the string?" Chris suddenly had this sick feeling. "Did you drop the ball of string?"

"I guess I put it down back where we found the car."

"That's just great. Now we have no idea how to find our way back." Todd couldn't believe he'd let this happen. How could he be so foolish?

"Which one of these tunnels did we come out of? Todd, I'm *really* scared. We've got to go back," said Jill.

The four of them stood there trying to determine which of the four tunnels they had just come out of.

Everyone had a different opinion; the tunnels all looked alike in the shadowy darkness of the mine.

"Let's find some way to mark each of these tunnels so that we'll be able to tell them apart," suggested Chris. "If we go down the wrong one, we can at least come back here and, one by one, try the others."

"Good idea, Chris. What can we use to mark them?"

"How 'bout candy wrappers?" Jill suggested. So together they came up with a different wrapper to mark each tunnel.

"Shall we try the Snickers tunnel, the Nestlé Crunch tunnel, or the Hershey's tunnel? I think we came through one of them."

CHOICE ⇒

If the group takes the Snickers tunnel, turn to page 25.

If the group takes the Hershey's tunnel, turn to page 139.

"**Y**eah, let's get out of here. No telling what those guys are up to," Chris said.

The group started back the way they had come, with Scotty leading. They soon came to the rope ladder and climbed up and back into Scotty's backyard, one by one.

"Thanks, Scotty, for the tour." The group caught the shuttle and made their way back to Todd's Nevada City home. He had managed to take care of their fixation on gold mines without getting himself or anyone else in trouble. He should have been pleased.

But as Todd lay in bed that night, he couldn't help wondering what those men had been doing digging in that tunnel. When it hit him, he couldn't believe how stupid he had been. "Chris, wake up."

"Whadeyawant?" Chris said, trying to shake the cobwebs out of his sleepy brain. He peered at his clock, then frowned at Todd. "It's almost two in the morning," he said with a sleepy scowl. "What do you want?"

Todd whispered. "Chris, we've got to go back."

"Back *where?*"

"To the tunnel. I think I know what those guys were doing. I only hope we're not too late."

Todd didn't dare wake up anyone at his house. After all, how would he explain that he'd taken everyone into a mine shaft? He and Chris managed to get out of the house quietly and get two bikes from the garage. Together they began to pedal the three miles over to Grass Valley.

Knock, knock, knock. Todd rapped on Scotty's window until the kid came to open it.

"What are you doing? Is that you, Todd?"

Todd quickly talked Scotty into leading them back down into the tunnels. He just knew that he had it figured out. But were they too late?

When they arrived at the place where the glowing Coleman lantern hung, they couldn't hear anything. The men seemed to have gone. Slowly, they approached the newly dug tunnel. What they saw staggered them.

On the floor, on top of a large blanket, sat piles of gold from the vault in the Gold Exchange. Todd had been right. They had tunneled up into the vault through the floor, where there wasn't any motion detector, and they had cleaned it out.

"We've got to tell the police," Scotty said under his breath.

"But where are the men?" Chris asked. "They wouldn't just leave all this gold here."

"They must be carrying a load to the surf—" Todd stopped. "Listen! I hear them. Let's get out of here."

CHOICE ⇉

If they go back the way they came, turn to page 39.

If they try to hide, turn to page 5.

"We better get out," said Todd. "We must be a mile downriver."

They pulled out and began the difficult walk back upriver. None of them had thought to bring their sandals, and there didn't seem to be any trail, so they found the going a bit rough on their feet.

"Which way?" Nancy asked, as they came to a place where the river's edge became a high ridge looming overhead. There seemed no place to walk but up the hill.

"Gotta go inland. There's no other way around this hill," Todd announced. Nancy and Jill led the group as Todd and Chris followed lugging the raft. Slowly they trudged through the low growth and up the hill.

This side of the river had more dry brush and the less vibrant digger pines. Todd always wondered why one slope of the Yuba Valley had different growth than the other. After they reached the top of the ridge and started down toward the river once again, they passed into a lush area of plants that suddenly made Todd uncomfortable.

"Ohhiee!" Jill tripped over a wire and fell into several of those bushes. The wire caused several bells to ring, as if she had set off somebody's alarm.

Todd dropped the raft and picked up Jill.

"Come on! Let's get back down to the river," he said with urgency.

"My ankle, I think I twisted it. What are all those bells for?"

You'll find out soon enough, Todd thought to himself. "Keep low and follow me," he ordered the others. He had Jill put her arm up on his shoulder so he could give her some support.

They started down the hill while Chris and Nancy followed quickly behind. When they had reached the river, Todd encouraged everyone to keep moving.

"Wait! My ankle hurts too much."

"We can't wait," he said, pushing them farther upriver.

"What is this all about?" Jill said at last, refusing to move any farther. "My ankle hurts too much."

"You stumbled over a trip wire on a marijuana farm. Those bells were to alert someone that we were in his plants. Those boys are 'bout as friendly as the miners when you get near their claims."

Jill's eyebrows arched. "You mean they grow that stuff right out here?"

"There are all sorts of mini-farms like that here and deeper up toward the North San Juan area. Those guys are paranoid of anyone walking through. For all they know you could be a sheriff. Or you could be just trying to rip off their plants. They might not be nearby, but no sense hanging around to find out."

Jill's ankle didn't seem that bad, so they continued up the river. As they walked, Jill felt angry that "her wilderness" had marijuana growing in it. That stuff certainly caused enough problems in big cities like Washington. "We should call the police and tell them what

134

we saw back there," she said with determination. They all agreed that would be a good idea; none of them admitted they were scared, though.

By the time they had reached Bridgeport, everyone's shoulders were getting red with sunburn. Todd knew the time had arrived for him to call home to get them picked up. Besides being tired and burned, they had a marijuana farm to report. They would have to look for gold on some other day.

THE END

But you can look for gold now. If you haven't already found it, turn back to page 1 and make other choices along the way.

Or, turn to page 143.

"**W**ell, if I have a choice, I would prefer to ride in a
car. But if you want, we can ride bicycles."

As soon as Jill spoke, Todd said, "No problem. We can
work that out." He leaned his bike against the redwood
beam holding up the deck and walked back inside the
house. In a moment, he came out of the attached garage
with a small two-man rubber raft and an inner tube.

"Let's get in the car. Mom said she'll take us to
Bridgeport. She's making us a picnic lunch because it's so
much farther down the river, and we'll probably get back
later."

"Bridgeport?" Chris looked confused. "I thought that
was in Connecticut."

"Naw, it's a place on the lower Yuba where there's an
old covered bridge."

"OK," Nancy said as she grabbed the tube and raced
for the car.

After thirty-five minutes the group reached the river.
Mrs. Winfield dropped them all off and said either she or
Todd's older brother, Ron, would pick them up at 4:00.

Todd and Chris carried the raft. Jill carried the lunch,
and Nancy held onto the inner tube as if she feared
someone might steal it from her. Together they made their
way down the path to a nice beach. Several other bathers

136

had already staked out claims on the white sand, and a few children played at the water's edge.

As they laid out their towels, Jill looked up at the large wooden bridge spanning the river. "That bridge is neat. They use it anymore?"

"Naw. It's just for looks now. Wanna explore it?"

"Hey, let's get in the water," Nancy suggested, jumping and sending her pigtails flopping.

"I thought you said we'd be seeing where all the gold came from?" Chris complained.

"There's always time for that, Chris. Relax and enjoy yourself. Right now our choices are tubing and bridge exploring."

CHOICE ⇒

If they decide to explore the bridge, turn to page 22.

If they go tubing, turn to page 13.

"**Y**ou're not scared, are you?" he questioned her.

"Oh, of course not. Why should I be scared?"

"Well, here," he said holding out his hand. "Let's do it."

She took his hand, wondering what she must be thinking of, and stepped off into the air.

Sp-lash!

The cold water made Jill feel she must be dying. She couldn't believe the water could be this cold, especially in July. "Oh-oh!" she cried as she swam quickly toward the edge of the natural pool.

"Great, huh?" Todd smiled. Jill tried not to let on how cold she felt.

For quite a while they both sat on a rock without talking. Finally, she said, "Will you miss me when we go back east?"

Her question took Todd by surprise. "Yeah," he admitted, looking the other way. "I wish ya didn't have to go back."

"Me, too."

After awhile, they went back up the river. Jill wondered if she should say anything to Todd about her being a Christian. *He should know,* she thought. And she should find out if he knew the Lord. But she couldn't think of how to say it so it sounded right.

Chris and Nancy were glad to see them when they

138

returned. Nancy wasn't feeling well, and Jill noticed that her face had swollen a little. Jill got concerned. It was time to head back to the road anyway so they could be picked up by Todd's brother.

Jill decided to write to Todd once she returned home. Maybe that would be how she could tell him about Jesus.

THE END
Turn to page 143.

"**I**'m sure we came from that direction," Chris said, pointing toward the tunnel marked with the Hershey's wrapper. The group followed him silently. They hadn't walked too far before the tunnel they were in started to go down steeply.

"I don't remember coming up any grade like this," said Nancy.

"It's really hard to tell what the grade is like under the ground. It's so hard to judge." But Todd realized that they were certainly going down fast.

"I'm sure this is it. Let's just go a little farther." Chris always wanted to keep going.

They turned a corner, and Todd's flashlight started reflecting light back at them. "What's this?" He took a few more steps and then stopped. "Water. We've hit water. The tunnel ahead is filled with water. We're going the wrong way."

Most of the group got pretty depressed as they turned back. Everyone wondered if they would ever see the light of day again.

As they walked back up, they suddenly came to a split in the tunnel.

"Oh no! I don't remember this. I never noticed that there was another shaft coming in."

140

"Now which way?" Jill said. Her thin body shivered uncontrollably.

"We're lost! We'll never get out!" Nancy sat down and burst into tears.

"Hey, we'll find our way out. We just have to be patient. We can't get all panicky." Todd didn't feel as reassuring as he hoped he sounded. "We only have two choices here. Left or right."

CHOICE ⇒

If they try the left tunnel, turn to page 55.

If they try the right tunnel, turn to page 111.

"**D**on't even think about running," the man said in a tough voice, guessing what they were thinking. "Go back into the mine."

This guy must be the lookout, thought Chris. The man spoke into his radio, and soon the boys came face-to-face with the other two thieves.

"You kids sure picked a bad time to go exploring," said a man with a voice that sounded as rough as gravel. Todd thought he'd seen the man's face before.

"What should we do with them, boss?" The skinny man looked at Todd for a minute, then moved his eyes around in a nervous way. He kept fingering his gun.

"Let's use 'em to help us carry out the rest of the loot," suggested the lookout.

The boss nodded. "Get in there!" he yelled, pushing Todd into the area where they had laid out their treasure. All six of them grabbed a portion of the remaining gold and carried it to the outside entrance. It didn't take long to load up the camper shell on their one-ton pickup.

"Now get in there with the gold!" said the gruff-voiced man as the three kids climbed into the camper shell. Suddenly Todd realized where he'd seen that face before. The man had worked at Mickey's Hamburgers in downtown Grass Valley.

142

The truck drove out of the city and traveled west toward Nevada County Airpark.

"What do you think they'll do with us?" Chris asked, his voice quivering.

"I don't know," Todd said, "but I recognized one of them. He used to work at Mickey's."

"Yeah!" Scotty perked up. "I remember him."

"Whatever you do, Scotty, don't let them know you recognize anyone."

The truck pulled out on the runway near a small airplane. Above the dark trees on the east they could just make out the faint blue sky of the approaching morning.

The men opened the camper shell and ordered the three kids to help load the airplane. Todd kept wondering what would happen when they had finished. The men didn't talk at all; they must have decided the kids' fate while riding out from town.

When they put the last bar of gold in the plane, the boss motioned to the skinny guy. He smiled and waved his gun at the three kids. "Move it!"

They did as he commanded, but Todd got a terrible sick feeling in his stomach. This felt like it might be an execution. He had an overpowering urge to yell, "Run!"

CHOICE ➡️

If they run, turn to page 65.

If they do as they're told, turn to page 53.

The vacation week that Jill and the Martin kids spent in the California gold rush towns of Nevada City and Grass Valley turned out to be a lot different than what they expected! I'm sure you are curious to discover all of the possible choices they experienced. Don't hesitate to begin again and see if you can discover for yourself each new twist in *The Abandoned Gold Mine*.

You also won't want to miss any of the other stories in this exciting adventure series. Get to know the whole Ringer gang and their friends—Willy, Tina, Jim, Sam, and Pete. You may even decide you want to become a Ringer yourself!

John C. Souter is an author and church planter in northern California. He has written thirty-eight books, including the popular Campus Magazine series. He lives with his wife, Susan, and their three children.